KU-060-957

THREE BEDROOMS, ONE CORPSE

AN AURORA TEAGARDEN NOVEL

CHARLAINE HARRIS

Copyright © Charlaine Harris Schulz 1994

All rights reserved

The right of Charlaine Harris to be identified as the author
of this work has been asserted by her in accordance with
the Copyright, Designs and Patents Act 1988.

First published in Great Britain in 2010 by
Gollancz
An imprint of the Orion Publishing Group
Orion House, 5 Upper St Martin's Lane,
London WC2H 9EA
An Hachette UK Company

This edition published in Great Britain in 2012 by Gollancz

1 3 5 7 9 10 8 6 4 2

A CIP catalogue record for this book
is available from the British Library

ISBN 978 0 575 10376 4

Typeset at The Spartan Press Ltd,
Lymington, Hants

Printed in Great Britain by Clays Ltd,
St Ives plc

The Orion Publishing Group's policy is to use papers
that are natural, renewable and recyclable products and
made from wood grown in sustainable forests. The logging
and manufacturing processes are expected to conform to
the environmental regulations of the country of origin.

www.charlaineharris.com
www.orionbooks.co.uk

RD045397

Dumfries and Galloway Libraries, Information and Archives

AAN

1 5 AUG 2012 AN

0 6 SEP 2012 AN

2 7 SEP 2012 AN

2 2 OCT 2012 AN

2 5 MAR 2013 AN

0 8 APR 2013 AN

1 3 JUL 2013 ST

6 MAR 2014 WH

1 0 JUN 2014 KB

1 0 OCT 2014 LA

- 6 JUN 2015 KB

0 5 APR 2016

1 9 JUL 2016

2 7 OCT 2016

1 7 NOV 2016

2 8 DEC 2016

2 1 FEB 2017

1 8 JUL 2017

6 OCT 2017

- 3 AUG 2018

0 2 DEC 2019

2 7 FEB 2020

2 7 JAN 2022

DUMFRIES AND GALLOWAY LIBRARIES WITHDRAWN

TIME

Central Support Unit
Catherine Street Dumfries DG1 1JB
tel: 01387 253820   fax: 01387 260294
e-mail: libs&i@dumgal.gov.uk

Dumfries and Galloway
LIBRARIES
Information and Archives

CUSTOMER
SERVICE
EXCELLENCE

UK

24 HOUR LOAN RENEWAL ON OUR WEBSITE - WWW.DUMGAL.GOV.UK/LIA

'Delightful . . . Clearly focused plot, animated description of character and real estate and sparkling prose commend this breath of fresh air to all collections'   *Library Journal*

Also by Charlaine Harris from Gollancz:

SOOKIE STACKHOUSE

The Sookie Stackhouse novels are also available
in three omnibus editions

HARPER CONNELLY

LILY BARD

The Lily Bard novels are also available in an omnibus edition

AURORA TEAGARDEN

The Aurora Teagarden novels are also available
in two omnibus editions

Wolfsbane and Mistletoe (co-edited with Toni L.P. Kelner)
Many Bloody Returns (co-edited with Toni L.P. Kelner)
Crimes by Moonlight
Death's Excellent Vacation (co-edited with Toni L.P. Kelner)

My thanks to
Atlanta-area Realtor/broker Joanne Kearney,
who provided me with much helpful information.
If I have misused it, the fault is mine.

DUMFRIES & GALLOWAY LIBRARIES	
045397	
Askews & Holts	
A·15	

Chapter One

My career as a real estate salesperson was short and un-official, but not uneventful. It started in the lobby of Eastern National Bank at nine thirty on a weekday morning with my mother glancing at her tiny, expensive gold watch.

'I can't make it,' she said with controlled savagery. A person who couldn't manage her appointments was in-efficient in my mother's estimation, and to find herself coming up short in that respect was almost intolerable. Of course, her dilemma was not her fault.

'It's those Thompsons,' she said furiously, 'always late! They should have been here forty-five minutes ago! Late for their own house closing!' She stared down at her tiny elegant watch as if she could change its reading by the force of her will. Her slim crossed legs were jiggling with im-patience, one navy-pump-shod foot swinging back and forth. When she got up, there might be a hole in the bank's ersatz oriental carpeting.

I sat beside her in the chair I would vacate for Mrs Thompson, when and if she showed up. A couple standing up Aida Brattle Teagarden Queensland for their own house closing was simply amazing; the Thompsons were gutsy, or so rich they wore an impervious armor of self-assurance.

'What are you going to be late for?' I was eyeing her crossed legs enviously. My own legs will never be long enough to be elegant. Actually, my feet couldn't even touch the floor. I waved at two people I knew in the time in took my mother to answer. Lawrenceton was like that. I'd lived in this small Georgia town all my life, and figured I'd be here forever; sooner or later, I'd join my great-grandparents in Shady Rest Cemetery. Most days that gave me a warm, fluid feeling; just part of that ole southern river of life.

Some days it made me crazy.

'The Bartells. He's come in from Illinois as plant manager of Pan-Am Agra, they're looking for a "really nice home," and we have an appointment to see the Anderton house. Actually, they've been here, or he's been here, I didn't get the details – he's been here for three months living in a motel while he gets things lined up at Pan-Am Agra, and now he has the leisure to house-hunt. And he asked around for the best Realtor in town. And he called me, last night. He apologized beautifully for disturbing me at home, but I don't think he was really a bit sorry. I know the Green-houses were thinking they would get him, since Donnie's cousin is his secretary. And I'm going to be *late*.'

'Oh,' I said, now understanding the depths of Mother's chagrin. She had a star listing and a star client, and being late for introducing one to the other was a professional disaster.

Getting the Anderton house listing had been a real coup in this smallish town with no multiple-listing service. If Mother could sell it quickly, it would be a feather in her cap (as if her cap needed any more adornment) and of course a hefty fee. The Anderton house might truthfully be called the Anderton mansion. Mandy Anderton, now married and living in L.A., had been a childhood acquaint-ance of mine, and I'd been to a few parties at her house. I remembered trying to keep my mouth closed so I wouldn't look so impressed.

'Listen,' said Mother with sudden resolution, 'you're going to meet the Bartells for me.'

'What?'

She scanned me with business eyes, rather than mother eyes. 'That's a nice dress; that rust color is good on you. Your hair looks okay today, and the new glasses are very nice. And I love your jacket. You take this fact sheet and run along over there – please, Aurora?' The coaxing tone sat oddly on my mother, who looked like Lauren Bacall and acted like the very successful Realtor/broker she is.

'Just show them around?' I asked, taking the fact sheet hesitantly and sliding forward to the edge of the blue leather chair. My gorgeous brand-new rust-and-brown suede pumps finally met the floor. I was dressed so discreetly because today was the third day I'd followed Mother around, supposedly learning the business while studying for my Realtor's license at night. Actually, I'd spent the time daydreaming. I would much rather have been looking for my own house. But Mother had pointed out cleverly that if I was in the office, I'd get first chance at almost any house that came up for sale.

Meeting the Bartells might be more interesting than observing Mother and the banker going through the apparently endless paperwork-and-signature minuet that concludes a house sale.

'Just till I get there,' my mother said. 'You're not a licensed Realtor, so you can't be *showing* them the house. You're just there to open the door and be pleasant until I get there. Please explain the situation to them, just enough to let them know it's not my fault I'm late. Here's the key.

Greenhouse Realty showed the house yesterday, but one of them must have given it to Patty early this morning; it was on the key board when I checked.'

'Okay,' I said agreeably. *Not* showing a rich couple a beautiful house was bound to be much more entertaining than sitting in a bank lobby.

I stuffed my paperback into my purse, put the Anderton key on my key ring, and kept a safe grip on the fact sheet.

'Thanks,' Mother said suddenly.

'Sure.'

'You really are pretty,' she said unexpectedly. 'And all the new clothes you bought are so much better than your old wardrobe.'

'Well . . . thanks.'

'Since Mary Elizabeth Mastrantonio was in that movie, your hair seems to strike people as fashionable rather than unmanageable. And,' she went on in an unprecedented burst of candor, 'I've always envied you your boobs.'

I grinned at her. 'We don't look like mother and daughter, do we?'

'You look like my mother, not me. She was an amazing woman.'

My mother had stunned me twice in one morning. Talking about the past was something she just didn't do. She lived in the here and now.

'Are you feeling okay?' I asked nervously.

'Yes, fine. I just noticed a little more gray this morning.'

'We'll talk later. I'd better get going.'

'Goodness, yes! Get over there!' Mother had looked at her watch again.

*

4

Luckily I'd met Mother at the bank instead of going with her from the office, so I had my own car. I got to the Anderton mansion in plenty of time to park to one side so my practical little car wouldn't mar the view from the curb. Two months ago, when old Mr Anderton had died, Mandy Anderton Morley (his sole heir) had flown in from Los Angeles for the funeral, put the house on the market the next day, and flown back out to her rich husband after clearing her father's clothes out of the master bedroom and emptying all the drawers into boxes that she had shipped to her home. All the furniture was still in place, and Mandy had indicated to my mother she would negotiate with the buyers if they wanted some or all of the furnishings. Mandy had never been a sentimental person.

So when I unlocked the double front doors and reached in to turn on the lights in the cold, stale two-storey foyer, the house looked eerily as it had when I was a child. I left the front doors open to let in some fresh air and stood just inside, looking up at the chandelier that had so awed me when I was eleven. I was sure the carpet had been replaced since then, but it seemed the same creamy color that had made me terribly conscious of any dust on my shoes. A huge brilliant silk-flower arrangement glowed on the marble table opposite the front doors. After you circled the marble table, you arrived at a wide staircase that led up to a broad landing, with double doors across from the top of the staircase echoing the double front doors below. I ran to turn the heat up so the house wouldn't be so chilly while I was not-showing it, and returned to shut the front doors. I flipped on the switch that lit the chandelier.

I had enough money to buy this house.

The realization gave me a tingle of delight. My spine straightened.

Of course I'd be broke soon after the purchase – taxes, electricity, etc. – but I actually had the asking price.

My friend – well, really, my friendly acquaintance – Jane Engle, an elderly woman with no children, had left me all her money and belongings. Tired of my job at the Lawrenceton Library, I'd quit; tired of living in a row of townhouses I managed for my mother, I'd decided to buy my own house. Jane's house, which I now owned, just wasn't what I wanted. For one thing, there wasn't room for our combined libraries of true and fictional crime. For another, my old flame Detective Arthur Smith, with his new wife, Lynn, and their baby, Lorna, lived right across the street.

So I was looking for my own new home, a place just mine, with no memories and no nerve-racking neighbors.

I had to laugh as I pictured myself eating tuna fish and Cheez-Its in the Anderton dining room.

I heard a car crunch up the semicircular gravel drive. The Bartells were arriving in a spotless white Mercedes. I stepped out onto the large front porch, if you can call a stone-and-pillars edifice a porch, and greeted them with a smile. The wind was chilly, and I pulled my wonderful new fuzzy brown jacket around me. I felt the wind pick up my hair and toss it around my face. I was at the top of the front steps looking down at the Bartells as he helped his wife from the car. Then he looked up at me.

Our eyes met. After a startled moment I blinked and collected myself.

'I'm Aurora Teagarden,' I said, and waited for the inevitable. Sure enough, sleek, dark Mrs Bartell sniggered before she could stop herself. 'My mother is delayed, which she very much regrets, and she asked me to meet you here so you could begin looking. There's so much to see in this house.'

There, I'd done my mother proud.

Mr Bartell was about five-ten, forty-fiveish, prematurely white-headed, with a tough, interesting face, and was wearing a suit even I could tell was a major investment. His eyes, which I was trying hard to avoid, were the lightest brown I'd ever seen. 'I'm Martin Bartell, Miss Teagarden,' he said in an unaccented Voice of Command, 'and this is my sister, Barbara Lampton.'

'Barby,' said Barbara Lampton with a girlish smile. Ms Lampton was maybe forty, broad in the beam but camouflaging it very skillfully, and not altogether happy at being in Lawrenceton, Georgia, pop. 15,000.

I raised my eyebrows only very slightly (after all, my mother wanted to sell this house). A Barby was laughing at an Aurora? And she wasn't Mrs Bartell, after all. But was she really his sister?

'Nice to meet you,' I said neutrally. 'Now, I'm not really showing you this house, I'm not a licensed Realtor, but I do have the fact sheet here in case you have any questions, and I am familiar with the layout and history of the house.'

So saying, I turned and led the way before Martin Bartell could ask why this was any different from showing the house.

'Barby' commented on the marble-topped table and the silk flowers, and I explained about the furniture.

To the right of the foyer, through a doorway, was a very sizable formal living room and a small formal dining room, and to the left the same space was divided into two large rooms, a 'family room' and a room that could be used for just about anything. Martin Bartell examined everything very carefully and asked several questions I was quite unable to answer, and a few I was.

I was careful always to be looking down at the fact sheet when he turned to ask me something.

'You could use this back room for your gym equipment,' Barby remarked.

So that was where the athletic movement and the muscles came from.

They wandered farther back and looked through the kitchen with its informal dining nook, then into the formal dining room, which lay between the kitchen and the living room.

Was his sister going to live with him? What would he do in a house this large? He would need a maid, for sure. I tried to think of whom I could call who might know of a reliable person. I tried *not* to picture myself in one of those 'French maid' outfits sold in the back of those strange confession magazines. (A junior-high girl left one in the library one time.)

All the time we were walking and looking, I kept in front of him, behind him, anywhere but facing him.

Instead of taking the kitchen stairs, I maneuvered Martin Bartell and Barby back to the main staircase. I had always loved that broad staircase. I glanced at my watch. Where was Mother? The upstairs was really the climax of the house, or at least I'd always thought so, and she should be the one to show it. Mr Bartell seemed content with me so far, but having me instead of Mother was like having hamburger when you'd been promised steak.

Though I had a very strong feeling Martin Bartell didn't think so.

This was turning out to be a complicated morning.

This man was at least fifteen years older than I, belonged to a world I hadn't the faintest inkling of, and was silently bringing to my attention the fact that for some time now I had been dating a minister who didn't believe in premarital sex. And before Father Aubrey Scott, I hadn't dated anyone at all for months.

Well, I couldn't keep them standing in the foyer while I reviewed my sex life (lack of). I mentally cracked a whip at my hormones and told myself I was probably imagining these waves of interest that washed over me.

'Up these stairs is one of the nicest rooms in the house,' I said determinedly. 'The master bedroom.' I looked at Mr Bartell's chin instead of his eyes. I started up, and they followed obligingly. He was right behind me as I mounted the stairs. I took a few deep breaths and tried to compose myself. Really, this was *too stupid*.

'There are only three bedrooms in this house,' I explained, 'but all of them are marvelous, really almost suites. Each has a dressing room, a walk-in closet, and a private bathroom.'

'Oh, that sounds wonderful,' said Barby.

Maybe they really *were* brother and sister?

'The master bedroom, which is behind these double doors at the head of the stairs, has two walk-in closets. The blue bedroom is the door on the right end of the landing, and the rose bedroom is the one on the left. The extra door to the left is to a small room the Andertons used as a homework and TV room for the children. It would be a good office, or sewing room, or . . .' I trailed off. The room was useful, okay? And it would be much more suitable for Martin Bartell's exercise equipment than a downstairs, public, room. 'The extra door to the right leads to the stairs that come up from the kitchen.'

All the bedroom doors were closed, which seemed a little odd.

On the other hand, the situation gave me a great dramatic moment. I turned both knobs simultaneously, swept open the master bedroom doors, and instantly moved to one side to give Mother's clients an unobstructed view while I glanced back to get their reaction.

'Oh, my *God*!' said Barby.

It wasn't what I'd expected.

Martin Bartell looked very grim.

Slowly and reluctantly, I turned to see what they were staring at.

The woman in the middle of the huge bed was sitting propped up against the headboard, with the white silk sheets pulled up to her waist. Her bare breasts shocked the eyes first; then her face, dark and swollen. The teased and disheveled black hair had been smoothed back to some semblance of normality. Her wrists, positioned at her sides, had some leather thongs around them.

'That's Tonia Lee Greenhouse,' remarked my mother from behind her clients. 'Aurora, please go make sure Tonia Lee is dead.'

That's my mother. Always say 'please', even when you're asking someone to check the vital signs of an obvious corpse. I had touched a dead person before, but it was not an experience I wanted to repeat. However, I had taken a step forward before a strong hand closed around my wrist.

'I'll do it,' Martin Bartell said unexpectedly. 'I've seen

dead people before. Barby, go downstairs and sit in that big front room.'

Without a word, Barby did as she was told. The Voice of Command even worked on a sister. Mr Bartell, his shoulders stiff, strode across the wide expanse of peach carpet and leaned across the huge bed to put his fingers to the neck of the very deceased Tonia Lee Greenhouse.

'As you can tell, she's definitely dead and has been for a while,' Mr Bartell said matter-of-factly enough. His nose wrinkled, and I knew he was getting a much stronger whiff than I of the very unpleasant smell emanating from the bed. 'Are the phones hooked up?'

'I'll see,' said Mother briefly. 'I'll try the one downstairs.' She spoke as if she'd decided that on a whim, but when I turned to look at her, her face was completely white. She turned with great dignity, and as she went down the stairs, she began to shake visibly – as though an earthquake only she could feel was rocking the staircase.

My feet had grown roots into the thick carpet. Though I wished myself somewhere else, I seemed to lack the energy to take me there.

'Who was this woman?' asked Mr Bartell, still bending over the bed but with his hands behind him. He was scrutinizing her neck with some detachment.

'Tonia Lee Greenhouse, half of Greenhouse Realty,' I said. It was a little surprising to hear my own voice. 'She showed this house yesterday. She had to get the key from my mother's office, but it was back there this morning.'

'That's very remarkable,' Mr Bartell said unemphatically.

And it surely was.

I stood there rooted, thinking how atypically everyone was behaving. I would have put money on Barby Lampton screaming hysterically, and she hadn't squeaked after her first exclamation. Martin Bartell hadn't gotten angry with us for showing him a house with a corpse in it. My mother hadn't ordered me to go downstairs to call the police, she'd done it herself. And instead of finding a solitary corner and brooding, I was standing stock-still watching a middle-aged businessman examine a naked corpse. I wished passionately I could cover up Tonia Lee's bosom. I stared at Tonia Lee's clothes, folded on the end of the bed. The red dress and black slip were folded so neatly, so oddly, in tiny perfect triangles. I brooded over this for some moments. I would have sworn Tonia Lee would be a tosser rather than a folder. And any dress subjected to that treatment would be a solid mass of wrinkles when it was shaken out.

'This lady was married?'

I nodded.

'Wonder if her husband reported her missing last night?' Mr Bartell asked, as if the answer would be interesting, no more. He straightened up and walked back over to me, his hands in his pockets as though he were passing the time until an appointment.

My brain was not moving so very quickly. I finally realized he was doing his best not to touch anything in the room.

'I'm sure we shouldn't cover her up,' I said wistfully. For once, I was wishing I hadn't read so much true and fictional crime, so I wouldn't know I was not supposed to adjust the corpse.

Martin Bartell's light brown eyes looked at me very thoroughly. They had a golden touch, like a tiger's.

'Miss Teagarden.'

'Mr Bartell . . . ?'

His hand emerged from his pocket and moved up. I tensed as though I were about to be jolted by electricity. I lost the technique of staring at his chin and looked right at him. He was going to touch my cheek.

'Is the body in here?' asked Detective Lynn Liggett Smith from perhaps three feet away.

Downstairs, at least thirty minutes later, I had recovered my composure. I no longer felt as if I was in heat and would rip Martin Bartell's clothes off any minute. I no longer felt that he, out of all the people in the world, had the power to look underneath all the layers of my personality and see the basic woman, who had been lonely (in one particular way) for a very long time.

In the 'family room,' with my mother and Barby Lampton to provide protective chaperonage, I was able to collect all my little foibles and peculiarities back together and stack them between myself and Martin Bartell.

My mother felt obligated to hold polite conversation with her clients. She had introduced herself formally, gotten over her surprise on finding out that Mr Bartell's companion was his sister, not his wife, and had established the fact that Martin Bartell had received good impressions of Lawrence-ton in the weeks he'd spent here. 'It's been a pleasant change of pace after the Chicago area,' he said, and sounded sincere. 'Barby and I grew up on a farm in a very rural area of Ohio.'

Barby didn't seem to enjoy being reminded.

He explained a little about his reorganization of the local Pan-Am Agra plant to my mother, a born manager, and I kept my eyes scrupulously to myself.

We waited for the police for a long time, it seemed. I

heard familiar voices calling up and down the stairs. I'd dated Lynn Liggett's husband, Arthur Smith (before they married, of course), and during our 'courtship' I'd become acquainted with every detective and most of the uniforms on Lawrenceton's small force. Detective Henske's cracker drawl, Lynn's crisp alto, Paul Allison's reedy voice . . . and then came the sound I dreaded.

Detective Sergeant Jack Burns.

I turned in my chair to group myself protectively with the other three. What were they talking about now? Martin Bartell had said he'd been at work every day of the three months he'd spent in Lawrenceton, and had invited Mother to tell him about the town. He couldn't have asked anyone more informed, except perhaps the Chamber of Commerce executive, a lonely man who worked touchingly hard to persuade the rest of the world to believe in Lawrenceton's intangible advantages.

I listened once more to the familiar litany.

'Four banks,' Mother enumerated, 'a country club, all the major automobile dealerships, though I'm afraid you'll have to get the Mercedes repaired in Atlanta.'

I heard Jack Burns shouting down the stairs. He wanted the fingerprint man to 'get his ass in gear'.

'Lawrenceton is practically a suburb of Atlanta now,' Barby Lampton said, earning her a hard look from my mother. Most Lawrencetonians were not too pleased about the ever-nearing annexation of Lawrenceton into the greater Atlanta area.

'And the school system is excellent,' my mother continued with a little twitch of her shoulders. 'Though I don't know if that's an area of interest—?'

'No, my son just graduated from college,' Martin Bartell murmured. 'And Barby's girl is a freshman at Kent State.'

'Aurora is my only child,' Mother said naturally enough. 'She's worked at the library here for what – six years, Roe?'

I nodded.

'A librarian,' he said thoughtfully.

Why was it librarians had such a prim image? With all the information available in books right there at their fingertips, librarians could be the best-informed people around. About anything.

'Now she's thinking about going into real estate, and looking for her own home at the same time.'

'You think you'd like selling homes?' Barby said politely.

'I'm beginning to think maybe it's not for me,' I admitted, and my mother looked chagrined.

'Honey, I know this morning has been a horrible experience – poor Tonia Lee – but you know this is not something that happens often. But I *am* beginning to think I'll have to establish some kind of system to check on my female Realtors when they are out showing a house to a client we don't know. Aurora, maybe Aubrey wouldn't like you selling real estate? My daughter has been dating our Episcopalian priest for several months,' she explained to her clients with an almost-convincing casualness.

'Episcopalians have a reputation for being generally liberal,' Martin Bartell remarked out of the blue.

'I know, but Aubrey is an exception if that really is true,' Mother said, and my heart sank. 'He is a wonderful man – I've come to know him since I married my present husband, who is a cradle Episcopalian – but Aubrey is very conservative.'

I felt my cheeks turn red in the cold room. I ran a nervous

hand under the hair at my neck, loosening the strands that had gotten tucked in my jacket collar, and tilted my head back a little to shake it straight.

Thinking about Tonia Lee Greenhouse was preferable to feeling like a parakeet that is extremely excited at the prospect of being eaten by the cat.

I thought about the loathsome way Tonia had been positioned, a parody of seductiveness. I thought about the leather thongs on Tonia's wrists. Had she been tied to the ornate wooden headboard? Old Mr and Mrs Anderton must be turning in their graves. I thought about Tonia Lee in life – tall, thin, with teased dark hair and bright makeup, a woman who was rumored to be often unfaithful to her husband, Donnie. I wondered if Donnie had just gotten tired of Tonia Lee's ways, if he'd followed her to her appointment and taken care of her after the client had left. I wondered if Tonia had been overcome by passion for her client and had bedded him here in the invitingly luxurious master bedroom, or if she'd had an assignation with someone she'd been seeing for a while. Maybe the house-showing had been a fictitious cover to let her romp in one of the prettiest houses in Lawrenceton.

'Mackie brought her the key yesterday,' I said suddenly.

'What?' asked my mother with reproof in her voice. I had no idea what they'd been talking about.

'Yesterday about five o'clock, while I was waiting for you in the reception room, Tonia Lee called your office and asked for the key. She said she'd been held up – if anyone was getting off work, she'd be really obliged if they could drop it off here; she'd meet them. I handed the phone to Mackie Knight. He was leaving just then, and he said he'd do it.'

'We'll have to tell the police. Maybe Mackie was the last one to see her alive – or maybe he saw the man she was going to show the house to!'

Then Jack Burns was in the doorway, and I sighed.

Detective Sergeant Jack Burns was a frightening man, and he really couldn't stand me. If he could ever arrest me for anything, he'd just love to do it. Luckily for me, I'm very law-abiding, and since I had come to know Jack Burns, I'd made sure I got my car inspected right on the dot, that I parallel-parked perfectly, and that I didn't even jaywalk.

'If it isn't Miss Teagarden,' he said with a terrifying affability. 'I declare, young woman, you get prettier every time I see you. And I always do seem to see you when I come to a murder scene, don't I?'

'Hello, Jack,' said my mother with a distinct edge to her voice.

'Mrs Teagarden – no, Mrs Queensland now, isn't it? I haven't seen you since your wedding; congratulations. And these must be our new residents? Hope you don't feel like running back north after today. Lawrenceton used to be such a quiet town, but the city is reaching out to us here, and I guess in a few years we'll have a crime rate like Atlanta's.'

Mother introduced her clients.

'Guess you won't want this house after today,' Jack Burns said genially. 'Ole Tonia Lee looked pretty bad. I'm sure sorry you all ran into this, you being new and all.'

'This could have happened anywhere,' Martin said. 'I'm beginning to think being a real estate agent is a hazardous occupation, like being a convenience-store clerk.'

'It certainly does seem so,' Jack Burns agreed. He was wearing a hideous suit, but I'll give him this much credit – I

17

don't think he cared a damn about what he wore or what people thought about it.

'Now, Mr Bartell, I believe you touched the deceased?' he continued.

'Yes, I walked over to make sure she was dead.'

'Did you touch anything on the bed?'

'No.'

'On the table by the bed?'

'Nothing in the bedroom,' Martin said very definitely, 'but the woman's neck.'

'You notice it was bruised?'

'Yes.'

'You know she was strangled?'

'It looked like it to me.'

'You have much experience with this kind of thing?'

'I was in Vietnam. I've had more experience with wounds. But I have seen one case of strangulation before, and this looked similar.'

'What about you, Mrs Lampton? You go in the room?'

'No,' Barby said quietly. 'I stayed on the landing outside. When Miss Teagarden opened the doors, of course I saw the poor woman right away. Then my brother told me to go downstairs. He knows I don't have a strong stomach, so of course it was better for me to go.'

'And you, Mrs – Queensland?'

'I came up the stairs just after Aurora opened the bedroom doors. I actually saw her swing them open from downstairs after I started up.' Mother explained about the Thompsons and her delegation of me to open the house for the Bartells. 'Excuse me, Mr Bartell and Mrs Lampton.'

'You're his sister,' Jack Burns said, as if trying to get that point quite clear. He swung his baleful gaze on poor Barby Lampton.

'Yes, I am,' she said angrily, stung by the doubt in his voice. 'I just got divorced, my only child's in college, I sold my own home as part of the divorce settlement, and my brother invited me to help him house-hunt down here out of sheer kindness.'

'Of course, I see,' said Jack Burns with disbelief written on every crease in his heavy cheeks.

Martin Bartell's hair might be white, but his eyebrows were still dark. Now they were drawn together ominously.

'When was the last time you saw Mrs Greenhouse, Roe?' Jack Burns had switched his questioning abruptly to me.

'I haven't seen Tonia Lee to speak to in weeks, and then it was only a casual conversation at the beauty parlor.' Tonia Lee had been having a dye job and a cut, and I'd been having one of my rare trims. She had tried the whole time to find out how much money Jane Engle had left me.

'Mr Bartell, had you contacted Mrs Greenhouse about looking at any homes?' Jack Burns shot the question at the Pan-Am Agra manager as though he would enjoy beating the answer out of him. What a charmer.

I could see Martin taking a deep breath. 'Mrs Queensland here is the only Realtor I have contacted in Lawrenceton,' he said firmly. 'And now, if you'll excuse me, Sergeant, my sister has had enough for this morning, and so have I. I have to get back to work.'

Without waiting for an answer, he got up and put his arm around his sister, who had risen even faster.

'Of course,' Burns said smoothly. 'I'm so sorry I've been holding you all up! You just go on, now. But please, folks, keep everything you saw at the scene of the murder to yourselves. That would help us out a whole bunch.'

'I think we'll be going, too,' my mother said coldly. 'You know where we'll be if you need us again.'

Jack Burns just nodded, ran a beefy hand over his thinning no-color hair, and stood with narrowed eyes watching us leave. 'Mrs Queensland!' he called when Mother was almost out the door. 'What about keys to this house?'

'Oh, yes, I forgot . . .' And Mother turned back to tell him about Mackie Knight and the key, and I walked out into the fresh chill of the day, away from the thing in the bedroom upstairs and the fear of Jack Burns.

And right into Martin Bartell.

Over his shoulder I saw Barby was in the front seat of the Mercedes and buckled up already. She was dabbing at her eyes with a tissue. She'd waited until she was outside to shed a few tears; I admired her control. I felt a sympathetic tear trickle down my own face. One way or another, the morning had been a dreadful strain.

I was looking at a silk tie in a shade of golden olive, with a white stripe and a thin sort of red one.

He wiped the tear from my face with his handkerchief, carefully not touching me with his fingers.

'Am I imagining this?' he asked very quietly.

I shook my head, still not meeting his eyes.

'We have to talk later.'

I couldn't speak, for once in my life. I was terrified of seeing him again; and I would rather have shaved my head than not see him again.

'How old *are* you? You're so tiny.'

'I'm thirty,' I said, and finally looked up at him.

He said after a moment, 'I'll call you.'

I nodded, and walked quickly over to my car and got in. I had to sit for a moment so I could stop shivering. Somehow I had his handkerchief clutched in my hand. Oh, that was just great! Maybe he had an old high school letter jacket I could wear? I was mad at my hormones, upset about the awful death of Tonia Lee Greenhouse, and horrified at my own perfidy toward Aubrey Scott.

There was knock on my window that made me jump.

My mother was bending, gesturing for me to roll the window down. 'I've never met Jack Burns in his professional capacity before,' she was saying furiously, 'and I pray I never do again. You told me he was like that, Aurora, but I couldn't quite credit it! Why, when I sold him and his wife that house, he was just so polite and nice!'

'Mom, I'm going to go to my place.'

'Why, sure, Aurora. Are you okay? And poor Donnie Greenhouse . . . I wonder if they've called him yet.'

'Mother, what you have to worry about, right now, is how that key got back on your key board. Someone at Select Realty put it there. The police are going to be all over your office asking questions just as quick as quick can be.'

'You definitely have a mind for crime,' Mother said disapprovingly, but she was thinking fast. 'It's that club you were in, I expect.'

'No. I was in Real Murders because I think that way, I don't think that way because I was in the club,' I said mildly. But she wasn't listening.

'Before I go back,' said Mother suddenly, 'I was thinking I should ask Martin Bartell and his sister – I can't believe a woman that age is answering to "Barby"—' This from a woman with a name like Aida. 'I should get them over to the house for dinner tomorrow night. Why don't you and Aubrey come?'

'Oh,' I said limply, horrified at the prospect. How was I going to excuse myself – 'Mom, this guy I just met, well, if we see each other again, we just may have at it on the floor'?

My mother, usually so sharp, did not pick up on my turmoil. Of course, she had a few more things on her mind.

'I know you have to ask Aubrey first, so just give me a call. I really think I should make some gesture to try to make up to them—'

'For showing them a house with a dead Realtor in it?'

'Exactly.'

Suddenly my mother realized that the Anderton house was going to be impossible to move, at least for a while, and she closed her eyes. I could see it in her face, I could read her mind.

'It'll sell sooner or later,' I said. 'It was too big for Mr Bartell anyway.'

'True,' she said faintly. 'The house on Ivy Avenue would be more appropriate. But if the sister is going to live with him, the separate bedroom suites would have been great.'

'See you later,' I said, starting my car.

'I'll call you,' she told me.

And I had no doubt she would.

Chapter Two

An hour after I'd gotten home I began to feel like myself again. I'd huddled wrapped in an afghan, with Madeleine the cat purring in my lap (an effective tranquilizer), while I watched CNN to feed my mind on impersonal things for a while. I was in my favorite brown suede-y chair with a diet drink beside me, comfortable and nearly calm. Of course, Madeleine was getting cat hairs all over the afghan and my lovely new dress; I'd had to resist the impulse to change into blue jeans when I got home. I still felt my new clothes were costumes I was wearing, costumes I should doff when I was really being myself.

I'd had Madeleine neutered after I'd given away the last kitten, and the scar still showed through her shorter tummy hair. She had quickly adjusted to the switch from Jane's house to the townhouse, though she was still angry at not being let outside.

'A litter box will just have to do until I find a house with a yard,' I told her, and she glared at me balefully.

I'd calmed down enough to think. I pushed the OFF button on the remote control.

I was horrified at what had happened to Tonia Lee, and I was trying very hard not to picture her as I'd last seen her. It was far more typical of Tonia Lee to remember her as she'd been at the beauty shop during our last conversation – her hair emerging glossy dark from the beautician's curling iron, her long oval nails perfectly polished by the manicurist, her brain trying to frame an impolite query politely, her dissatisfied face momentarily intent on extracting information from me. I was sorry she'd had such a dreadful end, but I'd never liked the little I knew of Tonia Lee Greenhouse.

Over and above being tangentially connected to her nasty death, I had a personal situation on my hands, no doubt about it. What had happened – and what was going to happen – between me and Martin Bartell?

I should call Amina, my best friend. Though she lived in Houston now, it would be worth the long-distance daytime call. I peered at the calendar across the room by the telephone in the kitchen area. Today was Thursday. The wedding had been five weeks ago . . . Yes, they should have gotten back from the cruise and the resort at least two weeks ago, and Amina wouldn't go back to work until Monday.

But if I called Amina, that would be validating my feeling.

So what was this feeling? Love at first sight? This didn't seem to be centered around my heart, but somewhere considerably lower.

And amazingly, he felt it, too.

That was what was so shocking – that it was mutual. After a lifetime of considering and dissecting, I was seriously in danger of being swept away by something I couldn't control.

Oh – sure I could! I slapped myself lightly on one cheek. All I had to do was *never see Martin Bartell again*.

That would be the honorable thing. I was dating Aubrey Scott, a fine man and a handsome one, and I should count myself lucky.

Which introduced a drearily familiar train of thought.

Where was my relationship with Aubrey going? We'd been dating for several months now, and I was sure his congregation (including my mother and her husband) expected great things. Of course, someone had told Aubrey about my involvement in the Real Murders deaths – due to my membership in a club devoted to discussing old murder cases, my half-brother Phillip and I had almost gotten killed – and we'd talked about it a little. But on the whole, other people seemed to consider our relationship suitable and unsurprising.

We found each other attractive, we were both Christians (though I was certainly not a very good one), neither of us drank more than the occasional glass of wine, and we both liked reading and popcorn and going to the movies. He enjoyed kissing me; I liked being kissed by him. We were fond of each other and respected each other.

But I would be a terrible minister's wife, inwardly if not outwardly. He must know that by now. And he wouldn't be right for me even if he was a – well, a librarian.

But I hated to do anything fast and drastic. Aubrey deserved better than that. My het-up feelings for Martin Bartell might disappear as suddenly as they'd appeared. And at least half of me fervently hoped those feelings would vanish. There was something degrading about this.

Also something terribly exciting, the other half admitted.

The phone rang just as I was about to go through my whole thought cycle again.

'Roe, are you all right?' Aubrey was so concerned it hurt me.

'Yes, Aubrey, I'm fine. I guess my mother called you.'

'She did, yes. She was very upset about poor Mrs Greenhouse, and worried about you.'

Maybe that wasn't exactly what Mother had been feeling, but Aubrey put the nicest interpretation on everything. Though he was certainly not naive.

'I'm all right,' I said wearily. 'It was just a tough morning.'

'I hope the police can catch whoever did this, and do it fast,' Aubrey said, 'if there's someone out there preying on lone women. Are you sure you want to go into this real estate business?'

'No, actually I'm not sure,' I said. 'But not because of Tonia Lee Greenhouse. My mother has to carry a calculator all the time, Aubrey.'

'Oh?' he said cautiously.

'She has to know all about the current interest rate, and she has to be able to figure out what someone's house payment will be if he can sell his house for X amount so he can put that down on the next house, which costs twenty thousand dollars more than the house he has . . .'

'You didn't realize that was involved in house-selling?' Aubrey was trying hard to sound neutral.

'Yes, I did,' I said, trying equally hard not to snap. 'But I was thinking more of the house-showing part of it. I like going into people's houses and just looking.' And that was the long and short of it.

'But you don't like the nuts and bolts part,' Aubrey prompted, probably trying to figure out if I was nosy, childish, or just plain weird.

'So maybe it's not for me,' I concluded, leaving him to judge.

'You have time to think about it. I know you want to do *something* – right?' My being completely at liberty, except for the nominal duty of listening to any complaints that might arise from the townhouse tenants in Mother's complex, made Aubrey very uneasy. Single women worked full-time, and for somebody other than their mothers.

'Sure.' He was not the only one who found the concept of a woman of leisure unsettling.

'Did your mother mention her plan for tomorrow night to you?'

Oh, *damn*. 'The dinner at her house?'

'Right. Did you want to go? I guess we could tell her we had already made other plans.' But Aubrey sounded wistful. He loved the food Mother's caterer served. 'Caterer' was a fancy term for Lucinda Esther, a majestic black woman who made a good living 'cooking for people who are too lazy', as she put it. Lucinda also got extra mileage out of being a 'character', a factor of which she was fully aware.

Oh, this was going to be awful. And yet, maybe it would clear the air in some way.

'Yes, let's go.'

'Okay, honey. I'll pick you up about six thirty.'

'I'll see you then,' I said absently.

'Bye.'

I said good-bye and hung up. My hand stayed on the receiver.

Honey? Aubrey had never called me an endearment before. It sounded to me as if something was happening with Aubrey . . . or maybe he was just feeling sentimental because I'd had a very bad experience that morning?

Suddenly I saw Tonia Lee Greenhouse as she had been in that huge bed. I saw the elegant matching night tables flanking the bed. I could see the strange color of Tonia Lee's body against the white sheets, the red of the dress folded so peculiarly at the foot of the bed. I wondered where Tonia Lee's shoes were – under the bed?

And speaking of missing things – here a thought hovered on the edge of my mind so insistently that my eyes went out of focus as I tried to pin it down. Missing things. Or something at least not included in my mental picture of the bed and surrounding floor. The night tables . . .

There it was. The night tables. My mental camera zoomed in on their surfaces. I picked up the phone and punched in seven familiar numbers.

'Select Realty,' said Patty Cloud's On-the-Ball voice.

'Patty, this is Roe. Let me speak to my mother if she's handy, please.'

'Sure, Roe,' said Patty in her Warm Personal voice. 'She's on another line – wait, she's off. Here you go.'

'Aida Queensland,' said my mother. Her new name still gave me a jolt.

'When you first listed the Anderton house,' I said without preamble, 'think about going in the bedroom with Mandy.'

'Okay, I'm there,' she said after a moment.

'Look at the night tables.'

A few seconds of silence.

'Oh,' she said slowly. 'Oh, I see what you mean. Yes, I have to call Detective Liggett right away. The vases are missing.'

'She should check the formal dining room, too. There was a crystal bowl with crystal fruit in there that cost a fortune.'

'I'll call her right away.'

We hung up at the same moment.

It had been years since I was at the Anderton house, but I still remembered how impressed I'd been that instead of tissues or bed lamps, Mandy's parents had Chinese vases on their bedside tables. In her charming way, Mandy had bragged about how much those vases had cost. But she had never liked them. So when I realized they were gone, I didn't for an instant think she'd had them packed up and shipped to Los Angeles. She would have left them to coax a buyer. Anyone who would have enough money to consider buying her parents' house would not want to steal vases, right?

I dumped an indignant Madeleine from my lap and moved around the room restlessly. I was standing at the window staring out at my patio, thinking I'd have to bring in my outdoor chairs and table and store them down in the basement during the coming weekend, when the phone rang. I reached out to the kitchen wall extension.

'It's me again,' said my mother. 'We're having a meeting this afternoon for everyone on the staff, two o'clock. You're going to need to come, too.'

'Did the police question Mackie?'

'They took him to the police station.'

'Oh, no.'

'It turns out Detective Liggett – I mean Detective *Smith* – was already here when I was on the phone with you. I'm sure this all happened as a result of what I told Jack Burns, about Mackie taking Tonia Lee the key. I was only thinking of Mackie having possibly seen who was at the house with Tonia Lee. It didn't occur to me until too late that they might pick up Mackie as a suspect.'

'Do you think it's because he's—?'

'Oh, I'd hate to think that. I hope our police force is not like that. But you know, being black may work in his favor, actually. Tonia Lee would never have gone to bed with Mackie. She didn't like blacks at all.'

'They might just say he raped her.'

There was a long pause while Mother digested this. 'You know, somehow it didn't . . . well, I can't say why. And I only looked for a second. But it didn't look like a rape, did it?'

I paused in turn. Tonia completely undressed, the sheets pulled back as if two people had actually gotten in the bed together . . . Mother was right, it looked like a seduction scene, not a hasty rape, even though the leather thongs might indicate force. My first thought had been consensual kinky sex. But maybe Mother and I were both factoring in Tonia Lee's known reputation for infidelity. When I suggested this to Mother, she agreed.

'Anyway, I'm sure Mackie is not involved,' she said staunchly. 'I like him a lot, he's a hard worker, and for the year he's been here, he's been totally honest and above-board. Besides . . . he is too smart to put the key back.'

After we'd hung up, I wondered about that. Why had the Anderton house key been put back on the hook so mysteriously? That key had enabled us to enter and find the body.

I thought a number of interesting questions depended on the answer to that riddle.

The office meeting ought to be stimulating.

I ate an apple and a leftover chicken breast while flipping through Jane Engle's copy of *The Murderers' Who's Who*. I read the entries for some of my favorite cases and wondered if an updated edition would include our local murderous duo whose dreadful but brief career had made national headlines; or perhaps our only other claim to fame might rate an entry, the disappearance of an entire family from a house outside of Lawrenceton. That had been – what? – five or six years ago.

My familiarity with old murder cases was my mother's despair. Now, since the disbandment of the Real Murders club, I had no one to share it with. I sighed over spilt milk.

After putting my dishes in the dishwasher, I glumly mounted the stairs to get ready for the meeting. For one thing, I had to brush all the cat hairs off my skirt.

Mother's office building, with its soothing gray and blue carpeting and walls, peaceful prints, and comfortable chairs, exuded calm and profitable efficiency. That was Mother's essence, and she and the office designer had captured it when they renovated the building. Mother had insisted on a conference room, for staff meetings. Every Monday every Realtor working for Mother had to attend this meeting. She'd planned to expand, and the room was still more than large enough for the whole staff.

I saw with interest that one of John Queensland's daughters-in-law had been brought in to answer the phones and take messages while Mother held the meeting. I knew my stepfather's sons and their wives only slightly, and as I nodded to Melinda Queensland, I tried to figure out what my relationship to her was. Stepsister-in-law? It looked to me as if I was going to be a stepaunt in a few months, but Melinda had had several miscarriages and I wasn't going to ask.

Melinda was sitting at Patty Cloud's desk, which of course was not only orderly but also decorated with a tidy plant and a picture in an expensive frame. Patty's desk faced the front door, and her underling, Debbie Lincoln, had a desk at right angles to it, in effect forming the start of the corridor down to the conference room and Idella's and Mackie's offices. In the square created by two walls and the desks, firmly screwed to the wall behind Patty, was the key board, a large peg-board striped with labeled hooks. The more popular letters of the alphabet claimed two or even three hooks. A person of even the feeblest intelligence could figure out the system in seconds, and every other agency in town had something similar.

I snapped out of my study of the key board to find that Melinda was waiting for me to acknowledge her, and her smile was growing strained as I stared at the wall behind her. I gave her a brisk nod and started down the hall to the conference room. I was in time to sit at Mother's left, a chair left vacant deliberately for me, I presumed. All the Realtors expected me to inherit this business from Mother, and saw my presence in the office this week as the first step in my becoming second-in-command.

This was far from true. I had quit my job at the library on a whim, and I already regretted it more than I ever would have believed possible. (Of course, even regretting it mildly was more than I ever would have believed possible.)

Idella Yates, a frail-looking fair woman in her mid-thirties, divorced with two children, slid into the chair at the end of the table and put a briefcase on the table in front of her as if building a barrier between herself and the room. Her short straight hair was the color of dead winter grass. Eileen Norris bustled in, carrying a large stack of papers and looking abstracted. Eileen was Mother's second-in-command, the first Realtor Mother had hired after she'd gone out on her own. Eileen was big, brassy, loud, and cheerful on the surface; underneath, she was a barracuda. Patty

Cloud, the receptionist/secretary, groomed to a tee, had perched her bottom dead in the center of the chair next to Idella's. Patty, who was maybe all of twenty-four, baffled and irritated me far more than she should have. Patty worked hard at being perfect, and she had damned near succeeded. She was always helpful on the phone, always turned out high-quality work, never forgot anything, and never, never came to work in anything frumpy or out of style or even wrinkled. She was already studying for her Realtor's license. She would probably pass at the top of her group.

Patty's underling, Debbie Lincoln, was a rather dim and cowed girl right out of high school. She was a full-figured black with hair expensively corn-rowed and decorated with beads. Debbie was quiet, punctual, and could type very well. Other than that, I knew little about her. At the moment she was sitting quietly by Patty with her eyes on her hands, not chatting back and forth like the others.

Eileen finally got settled, and we all looked at Mother expectantly. Just as she opened her mouth, the conference room door opened and in came Mackie Knight.

His dark round face looked strained and upset, and he responded to our various exclamations with a wave of his hand. He collapsed into a chair by Eileen with obvious relief, automatically adjusting his tie and running a hand over his very short hair.

'Mackie, I thought I was going to have to send a lawyer down to the station to get you out!'

'Thanks, Mrs Queensland. You were going to be my one phone call,' he said. 'But they seem to believe, at least for the moment, that I didn't do it.'

'What did happen yesterday?' Eileen asked.

We all leaned forward to listen.

'Well,' Mackie began wearily, telling a story he'd obviously told several times already, 'the phone rang here five minutes after Patty went home for the day, and I was standing out in the reception room talking to Roe, so I answered it.'

Patty looked chagrined that she hadn't worked late the day before.

'It was Mrs Greenhouse, and she said she had an appointment to meet a client to show him the Anderton house. She had forgotten to come by earlier to get the key – if anyone happened to be leaving our office soon, could they bring it by? She was worried she'd miss her client if she left to come to our office.'

'She didn't name the client?' Mother asked.

'No name,' Mackie said firmly. 'She did say "he", I'm almost positive.'

Idella Yates, beside me, shuddered and clutched her arms as if she were feeling a chill. I think we all did; Tonia Lee, making arrangements to meet her own death.

'Anyway, this is the part the police have the most trouble with,' Mackie continued. 'What I did, instead of driving up and leaving the key and going on home . . . I went home first, put on my jogging clothes, and went out for my run. I stuck the key in the pocket of my shorts and stopped on my run to hand it to Mrs Greenhouse. That only made maybe seven to ten minutes' difference in the time I actually got there, and it suited me better. To tell you the honest truth, I wasn't so excited about doing her work for her. No one here would be that sloppy. When I got there, she was at the house by herself. If anyone else was there, I didn't see him. Hers was the only car. It was parked in the back, outside the kitchen, so that was the door I went to.'

'Why does that seem funny to the police?' Mother asked. 'It doesn't seem odd to me.'

'They seem to think that I ran instead of driving my car so no one would identify my car as being in the driveway, later. They said a woman living across the street from the Anderton house, she was waiting for her daughter to get home from spending a week out of town. So she was sitting in her front room, looking out the window, and reading a book, for the best part of two hours . . . the daughter had had a flat on the interstate, turns out. This woman might have missed a person on foot, but not a car.'

'What about the back door?' Eileen asked.

'The people who live behind the Andertons were watching TV in their den with the curtains open, since they knew no one was in the Anderton house. They told the police that they saw Tonia Lee's car pull up when it was still daylight, but fading fast. One woman got out. They sat watching TV and eating in their den while they watched, and no other car ever pulled up. They figured someone else had come to the front door. They did see Tonia Lee's car pull out after dark, way after dark, but of course they couldn't see who was in it. They were pretty interested, someone being in the house for that long; they thought someone might really be thinking of buying.'

We all mulled that over for a minute.

'I wonder why the police told you so much?' Patty asked.

Mackie shook his head. 'I guess they thought they would pressure me into confessing or something. If I'd been guilty, it might have worked.'

'You run every night, you've always told us that, and I've often seen you. That's not suspicious at all,' my mother said staunchly. We all murmured agreement, even Patty Cloud, who was none too fond of having to do work for a black man, I'd observed. Though having Debbie working for *her* didn't seem to be a problem.

'Lots of people run or ride bikes in the evening,' Idella said suddenly. 'Donnie Greenhouse does . . . Franklin Farrell does.'

Franklin Farrell was another local Realtor.

'I bet it was Donnie,' Eileen said bluntly. 'He just couldn't stand Tonia Lee screwing around anymore.'

'Eileen,' Mother said warningly.

'It's true, and we all know it,' Eileen said.

'I'm sure she just made an appointment with someone who used a false name, and the man killed her,' Idella said in so low a voice we had to strain to hear her. 'It could happen to any of us.'

We were all silent for a moment, staring at her.

'Except Mackie, of course,' Eileen said briskly, and we all broke into laughter.

'Naw, I just get framed for it,' Mackie said after the last chuckle had died away. And we were all sober again.

Patty Cloud said suddenly, 'I think it was the House Hunter.'

'Oh,' my mother said doubtingly. 'Come on, Patty.'

'The House Hunter,' said Eileen consideringly. 'It's possible.'

'Who's that?' I asked. I was apparently the only one not in the know.

'The House Hunter,' Idella said softly, 'is what all the Realtors in town call Jimmy Hunter, the owner of the hardware store. On Main, you know?'

'Susu's husband?' I asked. There were several women named Sally in Lawrenceton, so most of them went by distinguishing nicknames. 'I was in their wedding,' I said, as if that made it impossible for Jimmy Hunter to be peculiar.

'We all know him,' Mother said dryly. 'And we christened him the House Hunter because he just loves to look at houses. Without Sally with him. He's always going to buy her a house for her birthday, or some such thing. And he's got the money to actually do it, that's the only reason we put up with him.'

'He's not really in the market?'

'Oh, hell no,' Eileen boomed. 'They're going to stay in that old house they inherited from Susu's folks till hell freezes over. He's just some mild kind of pervert. He just likes to look at houses.'

'With women,' Idella added.

'Yes, when we sent him out with Mackie, he didn't call us back for months,' Mother said.

'He won't make appointments with Franklin, either,' Idella added. 'Just that Terry Sternholtz that works with him.' Eileen laughed at that, and we all looked at her curiously.

'Maybe he called Greenhouse Realty instead,' Mackie said quietly.

'And since the Greenhouses are hard up, Donnie sent Tonia Lee out with him, just on the off chance he might really buy something.' This was Eileen's contribution.

'Let me get this straight. He doesn't make passes?' I asked.

'No.' Mother shook her head emphatically. 'If he did, none of us would show him a doghouse. He just likes to look through other people's homes, and he likes to have a woman who isn't his wife with him. Who knows what's going through his head?'

37

'How long has Jimmy been doing this?' I was fascinated with this bizarre behavior on the part of my friend's husband. 'Does Susu know?'

'I don't have any idea. How would any of us tell her? On the other hand, it does seem strange that gossip hasn't informed her that her husband is house-hunting. But as far as I know, she's never said anything. You were close to Susu in high school, weren't you, Roe?'

I nodded. 'But we don't see each other much nowadays.' I forbore from adding that that was because Susu was always ferrying her children somewhere or involved in some PTA activity. I was having trouble picturing thick-featured Jimmy Hunter, still broad-shouldered and husky as he'd been in his football days but now definitely on the heavyweight side, wandering dreamily through houses he didn't want to buy.

'If it's not the House Hunter,' Patty suggested, 'maybe Tonia Lee's murder has something to do with the thefts.'

This caused an even greater reaction than Patty's first suggestion. But this reaction was different. Dead silence. Everyone looked upset. Beside me, Idella rubbed her hands together, and her pale blue eyes brimmed with tears.

'Okay,' I said finally, 'fill me in on *this*. The real estate business in this town just seems to be full of secrets, these days.'

Mother sighed. 'It's a serious problem, not something like the House Hunter, whom we more or less treat as a joke.' She paused, considering how to proceed.

'Things have been stolen from the houses for sale for the past two years,' Eileen said bluntly.

Even Debbie Lincoln was roused by this. She slid her eyes sideways at Eileen.

'In houses just listed by a particular Realtor? In houses that have just been shown by one Realtor every time?' I asked impatiently.

'That's just the trouble,' Mother said. 'It's not like – say, the refrigerator vanished every time Tonia Lee showed a house. That would make it clear and easy.'

'It's small things,' Mackie said. 'Valuable things. But not so small a client could slip them into a pocket while we were showing the home. And even though the property might be listed with one Realtor, of course we let any other Realtor show it – that's the way you have to be in a town this size. We all have to cooperate. We all leave a card when we show a house, whether the owner's home or not . . . you know the procedure. If only we'd gotten the multiple-listing system, we could use lockboxes. None of this would have happened.'

What he meant was, none of the police station routine would have happened to *him*, because he wouldn't have had to take a key to the Anderton house. Tonia Lee would be just as dead, presumably. Mother was in favor of paying for one of the multiple-listing services most of the Atlanta area towns used, but the smaller Realtors in town – particularly the Greenhouses – had balked.

'And it was never the same people, never, any more than coincidence could explain,' Mother was saying. 'I don't think the houses had been shown by the same person – or to the same person – before the items were missed, any time.'

'You all borrow keys back and forth,' I said.

The Realtors nodded.

'So anyone could have them copied and use them at his or her leisure.'

Again, glum nods all around.

'So why haven't I read about this in the paper?'

Distinctly guilty looks.

'We all got together,' Eileen said. 'Us, Select Realty; Donnie and Tonia Lee, Greenhouse Realty; Franklin Farrell and Terry Sternholtz, Today's Homes; even the agency that deals mostly in farms, Russell & Dietrich, because we had shown some of the farmhouses.'

'City people who want to say they own property in the country,' Mother told me, raising her eyebrows in derision.

'And what happened at the meeting?' I asked everyone at the table.

No one seemed in any big hurry to answer.

'Nothing was settled,' Idella murmured.

Eileen snorted. 'That's putting it mildly.'

'Lots of mutual accusations and a general clearinghouse of old grievances,' Mother said. 'But finally, to keep this out of the papers, we agreed to reimburse the homeowner for anything missing while the house was listed.'

'That's pretty broad.'

'Well, there couldn't be any signs of a break-in.'

'And there never were?'

'Oh, token ones, and the police came in at first. That Detective Smith,' said Mother distastefully. She was unshakable in her conviction that Arthur Smith had done me wrong and that Lynn Liggett had somehow stolen him from my arms, despite the fact that Arthur and I had broken up before he began dating Lynn. Maybe a week before, it's true. And I'd only broken up with Arthur maybe twenty seconds before he was going to break up with me, so I could salvage some dignity. But what the hell . . . it was all over.

'And what did he find?'

'He found,' said Mother carefully, 'that in his expert

opinion, the break-ins were staged to cover up the fact that the thief had entered with a key. And later on, the thief didn't even pretend to break in.'

'But there was no one to accuse – any of us could have been guilty or innocent,' Mackie said. 'As usual, they checked me out first.' He wasn't disguising his bitterness.

'No one was showing any sudden affluence. No one was taking lots of trips to Atlanta to dispose of the stolen items, at least as far as he could tell. Of course, we all go to Atlanta often,' Eileen said. 'And I gather the Lawrenceton police force is not large enough to follow all the Lawrenceton Realtors wherever they go.'

Would Arthur tell me any more? I wondered. Had he, for example, staked out a house that might be robbed? Had he had any suspicions that he couldn't prove?

'As far as we know, the investigation is ongoing,' Mother said with apparent disbelief. 'The whole thing is still up in the air and has been for a long time, too long. We're all sick to death of watching our every move for fear it'll be misinterpreted. At least the talk about this isn't so widespread that people are afraid to list their houses, but it may come to that.'

'That would really hurt business,' Eileen said, and there was a reverent silence.

'So who,' I asked, moving on to the vital question, 'put the key back on the board?'

Chapter Three

That question had to be asked and answered sooner rather than later, and I stuck my neck out to ask it because I was very interested in the answer.

But you would have thought I was a policeman with a rubber hose, one who was furthermore holding their kids as hostages.

'We have to find out,' my mother said. 'Someone in this office got that key and put it back on the key board. No one here knew I was going to show the Anderton house this morning. I didn't know it myself until last night, when Mr Bartell called me at home. So it was likely the body wouldn't be found for a long time – how often do we show the Anderton house? Maybe one client in ten can afford a house like that.'

For the first time Debbie Lincoln opened her mouth. 'Someone,' she offered softly, 'could have come in when Patty and me were both gone from the reception area.'

Patty shot her a look. 'We're never supposed to both be gone from the reception area. But there was a period of maybe five minutes this morning when both Debbie and I were not there,' she admitted. 'While Debbie was in the back copying the sheet for the Blanding house, I had to visit the ladies' room.'

'I walked through while no one was there,' Eileen said

immediately. 'And I didn't see anyone coming in from outside.'

'So that narrows the time someone could have come in by a few more seconds,' I observed.

Mother said, 'It would have to be someone who knew our system and could find the right hook for the Anderton key very quickly.'

'Every Realtor in town knows where our key board is, and that we label every hook alphabetically,' Mackie said.

'So you're saying whoever returned the key is another Realtor, or one of you,' I pointed out. 'Though I think anyone coming into the office could figure out the key board in seconds. But it does make more sense for a Realtor to have returned it, to have realized *not* having the key on the board would have alerted us much sooner than the key being there. It's just bad luck for whoever killed Tonia Lee that Martin Bartell wanted to see some big houses this morning, and that he called Mother at home last night after the office was closed.'

Again I was aware of my lack of popularity as the people around the table realized they'd just been boxed in.

'All right,' said Patty defensively and illogically, 'where is Tonia Lee's car? Why wasn't it at the Anderton house this morning?'

That was another interesting question. And one I hadn't thought of . . . nor had anyone else in the room.

'It's parked behind Greenhouse Realty,' said a new voice from the door. 'And wiped clean of fingerprints.'

My old buddy Lynn Liggett Smith, making another of her silent entrances.

'Your daughter-in-law told me to come on back,' she told my mother, who had a particularly nasty gleam in her eye. I didn't think Melinda would be asked to answer the phones anymore.

Lynn was a tall, slim woman with short brown hair very attractively styled. She wore little or no makeup, always pumps or flats, and plain solid-color suits with bright blouses. Lynn was brave and smart, and sometimes I regretted that because of Arthur we would never be good friends. Lynn was also the only detective specifically designated 'homicide' at the Lawrenceton police department; she'd served on the Atlanta police force before taking what she thought would be a lower-stress job. She hadn't counted on Detective Sergeant Jack Burns.

'When did you find her car?' Mother was scrambling to regain her composure.

'This afternoon. Mr Greenhouse knew it was there this morning, but he didn't think that was important, because he thought Mrs Greenhouse had driven off in someone else's car. He just plain didn't know where Mrs Greenhouse was, and when she didn't come home last night, he thought she was just spending the night with someone else. I gather it's common knowledge she was prone to do that sort of thing.' Lynn had made a little pun, and she gave me the ghost of a smile.

'But today Mr Knight has told us that Mrs Greenhouse's car was in the driveway of the Anderton house last night, so she got there under her own steam. Someone, presumably the murderer, drove that car to Greenhouse Realty and left it there out of sight of the street.' Lynn cocked, her head and scanned our faces.

The absence of the car would have been noticed by Donnie Greenhouse, just as the absence of the key would have been noticed at our office, sooner or later.

But the murderer had had bad luck, no doubt about it.

'So,' Lynn continued, 'who put the key back?'

'My daughter brought that up, too,' Mother said smoothly. 'We have decided that at one point this morning, early, someone could have entered the reception area without being seen.'

'How long a time would this one point have lasted?'

'Five minutes. Or less,' Patty Cloud said reluctantly.

'No one wants to 'fess up, I guess,' Lynn said hopefully.

Silence.

'Well, I'll need to talk to each of you separately,' she said. 'If you all have finished your meeting, perhaps I could just stay in here? I'll start with you, Mrs Tea – No, Mrs Queensland. That okay?'

'Of course,' Mother said. 'Back to your work, the rest of you. But don't leave until the detective has a chance to talk to you. Rearrange your appointments.'

Beside me Idella Yates sighed. She picked up her briefcase and pushed back her chair. I turned to make some remark and suddenly realized Idella had been crying silently, something I have never mastered. I caught her eye as she dabbed at her cheeks with a handkerchief.

'Stupid,' she said bitterly. Feeling rather puzzled, I watched her leave the room. If Idella and Tonia Lee had been friends, it would have surprised me considerably. And Idella's reaction seemed a little extreme otherwise.

I made my own exit wondering where I would wait for my turn with Lynn. My mother's office, I decided, and started down the hall.

A young woman was standing in the reception area. I vaguely recognized her as I went through on my way to the left-hand corridor that led to Mother's office.

'Miss Teagarden?' she said hesitantly. I turned and smiled with equal uncertainty.

'I believe I met you at the church last week,' she said, holding out a slim hand. I jogged my memory.

'Oh, of course,' I said, none too soon. 'Mrs Kaye.'

'Emily,' she said, smiling.

'Aurora,' I told her, and to her credit, her smile barely faltered.

'Do you work here?' she asked. 'At Select Realty?'

'Not really,' I confessed. 'It's my mother's agency, and I'm trying to find out a little more about how the business works.' That was close enough to the truth.

Emily Kaye was at least five inches taller than I, no great feat. She was slim and small-breasted and dressed in a perfect suburban sweater and skirt and low-heeled shoes . . . and her purse matched, too. Her jewelry was small, unobtrusive, but real. Her hair was golden brown and tossed back from her face in a smooth, well-cut mane.

'Did you like the church?' I asked.

'Oh, yes, and Father Scott is so nice,' she said earnestly.

Huh?

'He is so good with children,' she went on. 'My little girl, Elizabeth, just loves him. He promised he'd take her to the park soon.'

He *what*?

All my senses went on full alert.

'You're so lucky,' she said.

My stare must have made her a bit nervous.

'To be dating him,' she added hastily.

So she'd been doing some research. I was thinking a number of things, so many that it would have taken a long time to have completed each thought.

Aubrey loved children? Aubrey had already visited his new parishioner and invited her little girl to the park?

'You play the organ, don't you?' I said thoughtfully.

'Oh, yes. Well, not very well.' She was lying through her teeth, I just knew it. 'I did play for the church in Macon.' Suspicion confirmed.

'You're – excuse me, you're a widow?'

'Yes,' she said briskly, to get quickly over a painful subject. 'Ken died last year in a car wreck, and it was hard to live in Macon after that. I don't have any family there, we were there just because of his job . . . but I do have an aunt, Cile Vernon, here in Lawrenceton, and she heard there was a teacher's job available at the kindergarten here, and I was lucky enough to get it. So now I'm house-hunting for a little place for Elizabeth and me.'

'Well, you came to the right Realtor,' I said, trying to brighten up the conversation and not give way to my deep suspicions. I had a feeling that if I looked over Emily Kaye's shoulder, I would see the writing on the wall for my relationship with Father Aubrey Scott.

'Yes, Mrs Yates is so nice. I'm really looking seriously at a little house on Honor right by the junior high school. It's just a couple of blocks from the kindergarten, and there's a preschool for my little girl nearby, too. Of course, I'd really like to quit work and stay home with Elizabeth,' she said wistfully.

That writing got darker and darker. *Sure* she would.

And to top it all off, that was my house, the house I'd inherited from Jane Engle, she was thinking of buying.

She'd be right across the street from Lynn and Arthur and their baby.

Aubrey would drop me and fall in love with this organ-playing widow with the cute little girl.

No, I was being paranoid.

No, I was being realistic.

'Mrs Kaye,' Idella's sweet voice said, just in the nick of time. 'I'm so sorry, we have to rearrange our appointment to see the house again.'

'Oh, and I had my aunt keep Elizabeth just so I could see it by myself!' Emily Kaye said, regret and accusation mingling in her voice.

I was battling a tide of rage and self-pity that had torn through me with the force of a monsoon. And I would rather have died than for Emily Kaye to notice that anything was wrong with me.

'Why don't you just go ask Detective Smith if you could run over for a half hour and show the house to Mrs Kaye?' I suggested to Idella, who was looking distressed at her client's disappointment. My voice rang a little hollow in my ears, and I felt my expression probably didn't match my concerned words, but I was doing the best I could.

'I'll do that,' Idella said with unaccustomed decision. 'Excuse me just a second.'

'Oh, thanks,' Emily told me with a warm sincerity that made me want to throw up. 'I hated to ask Aunt Cile to keep Elizabeth this morning. I don't want her to think I moved here just to have a free babysitter!'

'Think nothing of it,' I answered with equal sincerity. I wanted to get out of that room so badly my feet were itching. Any minute I was going to slap the tar out of Emily Kaye.

And why? I asked myself as I gave her a final, civil nod and glided off down the hall to Mother's office. Because, I answered myself angrily, Emily Kaye was going to get married, she would marry Aubrey, and even if I didn't want to marry him, I would once again be *left*. I knew I was being childish, I knew there was nothing logical about my feeling, and still I couldn't help it. This was not my finest hour.

It was time for one of my pep talks.

It is better not to be married than to be married unhappily.

Women do not need to be married to have rich, fulfilled lives.

I didn't want to marry Aubrey anyway, and I probably wouldn't have accepted if Arthur Smith had asked me. (Well, yes I would, but it would've been a mistake.)

All relationships fail until you find the right one. It's inevitable.

The failure of a relationship to lead to marriage does not mean you are unworthy or unattractive.

Having told myself all this, I recited the list again.

By the time Mother returned to her office, I'd completed the circuit three times. Mother was not in the best of humor, either. She was fuming about the disruption of the office, about being questioned again by the police, about the nerve of Tonia Lee, turning up dead in a Select Realty listing. Of course, she didn't use those words, but that was the gist of her diatribe.

'Oh, listen to me!' she said suddenly. 'I can't believe I'm going on like this, and a woman I know is probably lying on a table somewhere waiting to be autopsied.' She shook her head at her own lack of empathy. 'We'll just have to put up with all this. I wasn't crazy about Tonia Lee, God knows, but no one should have to go through what she must have.'

'You did tell Lynn about the thefts?'

'Yes. I let her draw her own conclusions. I'd already told her about the vases missing from the Anderton house. So I went on and told her about the pilfering that's been going on. Of course, it's more than pilfering. Someone in our little group of Realtors is seriously dishonest.'

'Mom, have you happened to think that Tonia Lee found out who stole the stuff from the houses? That maybe that was why she got killed?'

'Yes. Of course. I hope the thefts had nothing to do with the murder.'

'That would mean that a Realtor is the killer.'

'Yes. Let's just drop the subject. We don't know anything. It was probably one of Tonia Lee's conquests that did her in.'

'Probably. Well, I'm going to go home as soon as Lynn talks to me.'

'You don't have a feel for the business, do you?' Mother said reluctantly.

'I don't think so,' I said with equal regret.

She reached across her desk and patted my hand, surprising me for the second time today. We are not touchers.

'Excuse me,' Debbie Lincoln said from the doorway. 'That woman wants you, Miss Teagarden.'

'Thanks,' I said. I retrieved my purse from the floor and fluttered my fingers at my mother. 'See you tomorrow night, Mom, if not sooner.'

'Okay, Aurora.'

That night, after I'd taken my shower and wrapped myself up in a warm robe, something that had been picking at the edges of my mind finally surfaced.

I looked up a number in the little Lawrenceton phone book and dialed.

'Hello?'

'Gerald, this is Roe Teagarden.'

'My goodness, girl. I haven't seen you in a year, I guess.'

'How are you doing, Gerald?'

'Oh, pretty well. You know, don't you, that I've re-married?'

'That's what I heard. Congratulations.'

'Mamie's cousin Marietta came to help me clean out her stuff after Mamie – died, and we just hit it off.'

'I'm so glad, Gerald.'

'Is there anything I can do for you, Roe?'

'Listen, I heard a name today and I'm trying to pin a case to it. Think you can help me?'

'I'll sure give it a shot. It's been a long time since I've read any true crime. Mamie getting killed kind of made my interest in crime fade . . .'

'Of course. I'm being so stupid calling you . . .'

'But lately I've thought about taking it up again. So what's your question?'

'You were always our walking encyclopedia in Real Murders, Gerald. So here's the question. Emily Kaye?'

'Emily Kaye . . . hmmmm. A victim, not a killer, I remember that right off the bat.'

'Okay. American?'

'Nope. Nope. English . . . early this century, 1920s, I think.'

I kept a respectful silence while Gerald rummaged through his mental attic of old murder cases. Since Gerald was an insurance salesman, his interest in wrongful death had always seemed rather natural.

'I got it!' he said triumphantly. 'Patrick Mahon! Married man who killed and cut up his mistress, Emily Kaye. There were pieces of her all over the holiday cottage he'd rented; he'd tried several methods to dispose of the body. He'd bought a knife and saw before he'd gone down to the cottage, so the jury didn't believe his excuse that she'd died accidentally. Let me flip open this book, Roe. Okay . . . his wife, who'd thought he was fooling around, found a ticket to retrieve a bag from the train station . . . and in the bag was a woman's bloodstained clothing. She told the police, I believe. So they backtracked Mahon and found the body parts. That what you needed to know?'

'Yes, thank you, Gerald. I appreciate your help.'

'No trouble at all.'

The early Emily Kaye was certainly a far cry from the present-day Emily. I couldn't imagine the Emily I knew going to a cottage for an illicit vacation with a married man.

So a little niggling point had been settled. I knew where I'd heard the name.

But there was no one I could share this fascinating bit of information with, no one who would appreciate it. For the second time in one day, I regretted the disbanding of Real Murders. Call us ghouls, call us just plain peculiar, we had had a good time with our admittedly offbeat hobby.

What had happened to the members of our little club? Of the twelve, one would go on trial soon for multiple murder, another had committed suicide, one had been murdered, one had been widowed, one had died of natural causes, one had been arrested for drug trafficking (Gifford's unusual lifestyle had finally attracted the wrong attention), one was in a mental institution . . . on the other hand, LeMaster was still busy and prosperous with his dry-cleaning business, presumably, though I hadn't seen him since Jane Engle's funeral. John Queensland had married my mother. Gerald had remarried. Arthur Smith had gotten married. And I . . .

It seemed LeMaster Cane and I were the only ones who were basically unchanged in life condition in the eighteen months or so since Real Murders had had its last meeting.

Chapter Four

Friday morning I woke with that blank feeling I'd had lately. Nothing specific to do, nowhere particular to go. No one expected me anywhere.

Even though library funding cuts had meant I'd only been part-time, my work hours had shaped my week. I had an increasingly strong feeling I wouldn't be throwing my lot in with Mother's at Select Realty, so I wouldn't be studying for my real estate license.

Lying in bed drowsily was not such a pleasure if it wasn't illicit, even with Madeleine's heavy warm body curled up against my leg. Before, I'd used this time to map out my day. Now the time lay like a wasteland before me. I didn't want to think about the dinner party tonight, didn't want to feel again the alternating apprehension and attraction Martin Bartell aroused in me.

So I scolded myself out of bed, down the stairs, and popped an exercise video into the VCR after switching on the coffeepot. I stretched and bent and hopped around obediently, grudging every necessary minute of it. Madeleine watched this new part of my morning routine with appalled fascination. Now that I was thirty, calories were no longer burning themselves off quite so easily. Three times a week my mother, clad in gorgeous exercise clothes, went to the newly opened Athletic Club and did aerobics. Mackie Knight, Franklin Farrell, and Donnie Greenhouse, plus a host of other Lawrencetonians, ran or biked every evening. I'd seen Franklin's cohort, Terry Sternholtz, out 'power walking' with Eileen. My mother's new husband was a golfer. Almost everyone I knew did *something* to keep her muscles in working order and her body in the proper shape. So I'd succumbed to the necessity myself, but with little grace and less enthusiasm.

At least I felt I'd earned my coffee and toast, and my shower was a real pleasure afterward. While I was drying my hair, I decided that today I'd start looking at houses seriously. I needed a project, and finding a house I really liked would do. Jane's books and the few things from her house I'd wanted to keep were stacked in odd places around the townhouse, and I was beginning to feel claustrophobic. Mother had hinted heavily that Jane's dining room set would be welcome in her third bedroom for a short time only.

Of course, I'd have to go through Select Realty, and I didn't think I ought to have Mother showing me around. Eileen, Idella, or Mackie? Mackie could use the vote of confidence, I reflected, standing bent at the waist with my hair hanging down so I could dry the bottom layer. But though I didn't have anything against Mackie, I never had been too crazy about him, either. I didn't think it was because he was black or because he was male. I just wasn't that comfortable with him. On the other hand, Eileen was smart and sometimes funny, but too bossy. Idella was sweet and could leave you alone when you needed to think, but she was no fun at all.

After a moment's consideration, I chose Eileen. I phoned the office.

Patty said she wasn't in.

I looked up Eileen's home number and punched it with an impatient finger.

'Hello?'

'May I speak to Eileen, please?'

'May I tell her who's calling?'

'Roe Teagarden.' Who the hell was this? Eileen's personal home secretary? On the other hand, it wasn't exactly my business.

Eileen finally came on the line.

'Hi, Eileen. I've decided to start moving on finding a house of my own. Can you show me some, pretty soon?'

'Sure! What are you looking for?'

Oh. Well, four walls and a roof . . . I began speaking as I thought. 'I want at least three bedrooms, because I need a room for a library. I want a kitchen with some counter space.' The townhouse was definitely deficient in that department. 'I want a large master bedroom with a very large closet.' For all my new clothes. 'I want at least two bathrooms.' Why not? One could always be kept pretty for company. 'And not lots of traffic.' For Madeleine, who was weaving around my ankles, rumbling her rough purr.

'What price range do you have in mind?'

I was still talking to an investment banker about what I would have to live on if I didn't use any of Jane's capital. But I could buy the house outright and then invest the rest, or I could put the money from the sale of Jane's house down on the new place . . . I let all this swirl around in my head, and then an answer popped to the top of my brain, like the answer popping up to the window of a fortune-telling ball.

'Okay,' Eileen said. 'Seventy-five to ninety-five gives us some room. There are quite a few for sale in that range since Golfwhite closed its factory here.' Golfwhite – which, logically enough, manufactured golf balls and other golfing accessories – had closed its Lawrenceton factory and moved all its people who were willing to move to the larger factory in Florida.

'I don't really need anything awfully big or important-looking,' I told Eileen, assailed by sudden doubts.

'Don't worry, Roe. If you don't like it, you don't have to buy it,' she said dryly. 'Let's get a start tomorrow afternoon. I'll see what I can get lined up in that time.'

After I'd dressed in my lime green blouse and navy blue pants and sweater, I had nothing better to do than drop in on my old friend Susu Saxby Hunter. The house she'd inherited from her parents was in the oldest part of Lawrenceton. The house had been built in the last quarter of the previous century, and had charming high ceilings and huge windows, negligible closets, and wide halls, a feature I was especially fond of for some reason. Wide halls are a great location for bookshelves, and Susu was wasting a whole lot of prime space, in my opinion. Of course, she had other things to worry about, I found out that morning. In a house the age of hers, the heating and cooling bills were extortionate, drafts were inescapable, curtains had to be custom-made because nothing was of standard size, and all the electric wiring had had to be replaced recently. To say nothing of the antiquated toilets and tubs that Susu had just replaced.

'But you love this house, don't you?' I said, sitting across from Susu at her 'country pine' kitchen table. Susu's kitchen was so heavily 'country', including a pie safe in the corner (lovingly refinished and containing no pies whatsoever), that you expected a goose to walk in with a blue bow around its neck.

'Yes,' she confessed, putting out her third cigarette. 'My great-grandparents built it when they were first married, and then my parents inherited and they redid it, and now I'm redoing it. I guess I always will be. It's lucky Jimmy's in the hardware business! The only thing it would be better if he did is if he were a licensed electrician. Or had a fabric store. Want some more coffee?'

'Sure,' I said, reflecting I'd have to view the renovated bathrooms quite soon at this rate. 'How's Jimmy doing?'

Susu didn't look quite as happy as she had when discussing the house. 'Roe, since we've been friends a long time, I'll tell you . . . I'm not sure how Jimmy's doing. He goes to work, and he works hard. He's really built the business up. And he goes to Rotary, and he goes to church, and he coaches Little Jim's baseball team in the summer. And he goes to Bethany's piano recitals. But sometimes I have the funniest feeling . . .' Her voice trailed off uncertainly, and she stared down at her smoldering cigarette.

'What, Susu?' I asked quietly, suddenly feeling a return of my high school affection for this bright, blond, plump, scared woman.

'His heart's not in it,' she said simply, and then gave a little laugh. 'I know that sounds stupid . . .'

Actually, she sounded quite perceptive, something I'd never suspected.

'Maybe he's just having sort of an early midlife crisis?' I suggested gently.

'Of course, you're probably right,' Susu said, obviously embarrassed by her own frankness. 'Come see how I decorated Bethany's room! She'll be a teenager before I know it.

Roe, I expect her to tell me any day that she's started her *periods!*'

'Oh, no!'

And we oohed and aahed our way up the stairs to Bethany's pretty-as-a-picture room, still decorated with childish things like favorite dolls – but the dolls were sharing space with posters of sullen young men in leather. Then we viewed Little Jim's room, with its duck-laden wallpaper and masculine plaids. It seems to be the view of those who design 'male' decorations that the male DNA includes a gene that requires duck-killing.

Then we moved on to Sally and Jim's room, resplendent with chintz and framed needlework, an antique cedar chest, and ruffled pillows on the beds. A picture from their wedding hung by Sally's dressing table, one of the whole carefully arranged wedding party.

'There you are, Roe, second from the end! Wasn't that a wonderful day?' Susu's pink fingernail landed on my very young face. That face, with its stiff smile, brought that day back to me all too vividly. I had known exactly how unbecoming the dreadful lavender ruffled bridesmaid's dress had been, and my unruly hair was topped with a picture hat trailing a matching lavender ribbon. My best friend, Amina, also a bridesmaid, had fared much better in that get-up because of her height and longer neck, and her smile was unreserved. Susu herself, radiant in fully deserved white, was gorgeous, and I told her so now. 'That was the wedding of the year,' I said, smiling a little. 'You were the first of us to be married. We were so envious.'

The memory of that envy, the thrill of being the first, momentarily warmed Susu's face. 'Jimmy was so hand-some,' she said quietly.

Yes, he had been.

'Honey, I'm here for lunch,' bellowed a voice from downstairs. Susu's plump face aged again. 'You won't believe who's here, Jimmy!' she called gaily.

And down the stairs we tripped, stuck in a time warp between that picture-book wedding and the reality of two children and a house.

Jimmy Hunter quickly brought me back to the present. It had been a long time since I'd seen him close up, and he'd aged and coarsened. The basic goodwill that had always lain behind his character seemed to be gone now, replaced by something like confusion, laced with a dose of wondering resentment. How could Jimmy Hunter's life not be idyllic? he seemed to be wondering. What could possibly be missing? I'd always thought of him as an uncomplicated jock. I saw I would have to revise this assessment of Jimmy just as I'd had to correct my reading of his wife.

'You look great, Roe,' Jimmy said heartily.

'Thanks, Jimmy. How's the hardware business?'

'Well, it keeps us in hamburger, with steak on the weekends once in a while,' he said casually. 'How's the realty market in Lawrenceton?'

Of course everyone in town had heard by now I'd left the library, and heard and speculated about my legacy from Jane Engle.

'Kind of upset, right now.'

'You mean about Tonia Lee? That gal just didn't know when to quit, did she?'

'Oh, Jimmy,' Susu protested.

'Now, sugar, you know as well as I do that Tonia Lee would cheat on her husband any time it came in her head to do it. She just did it once too often, with the wrong man at the wrong time.'

As right as he might be, he said this in a very unpleasant way, a way that made me want to defend Tonia Lee Greenhouse. Jimmy was the kind of man who would say a woman deserved to get raped if she wore a low-cut blouse and tight skirt.

'She was unwise,' I said levelly, 'but she didn't deserve to be murdered. No one deserves to be killed for making some mistakes.'

'You're right,' said Jimmy, backing down instantly, though obviously not changing his opinion at all. 'Well, I can see you ladies have a lot to talk about, so I'll just take myself outside to work in the toolshed. Call me when lunch is ready, Susu.'

'Okay,' she responded warmly. When he was out the back door and down the steps, her face seemed to fold in.

'Oh, Roe, he's always going out to that toolshed! He's redone it as a workshop, and he spends hours out there piddling with this or that. He's a good husband as far as providing goes, and he loves the kids, but I just don't feel like he really lives here half the time.'

Caught unawares, I couldn't think of what to say. I patted her shoulder awkwardly, uncomfortable as usual when touching people.

'You know what he does?' Susu asked as she rummaged in the refrigerator and emerged with some leftover dishes. 'He goes and looks at houses! When we have this lovely home that I don't want to give up, ever! He just makes these appointments and looks at houses!' She popped the dishes in the microwave and punched in a time setting. 'I don't know how he explains to the Realtors that I'm never with him – I'm sure they expect his wife to come along if he's really house-hunting. I've had people whose homes were for sale ask me how Jimmy liked their house, and I didn't know anything about it!' Susu grabbed a tissue from a crochet-covered tissue box and blotted her eyes with ferocious intensity. 'It's so humiliating.'

'Oh, Susu,' I said with considerable distress, 'I have no idea why Jimmy would do that.' The microwave beeped, and Susu began pulling things out and then got two plates from the cupboard.

'I'll bet you've heard about it, though, haven't you?' She could tell my answer by my face. 'Everyone has. Even Bethany came home from school asking me if it was true her daddy was peculiar.'

'Maybe this house is just so much yours,' I said hesitantly. I knew it was stupid to open my mouth, but I did it anyway.

'Of course it's mine,' Susu said grimly. 'It's been my family's and it's in my name and I love it and it's going to stay that way.'

There seemed little more to say. Susu had drawn a line, and her husband was stepping over it, his fanciful house-hunting an odd symptom of a deep dissatisfaction.

Or at least that was the way I saw it. (I am as bad at practicing amateur psychology as anyone I know.)

I tried to get up and leave, having turned down repeated invitations to eat with them, but Susu determinedly kept me talking, though lunch was seemingly ready. She wanted us to talk about all the other bridesmaids. These reminiscences seemed to feed her something she needed. Naturally, all of them but me were married; some had been married more than once. Or twice.

'I heard you've been dating Aubrey Scott,' Susu said encouragingly.

'We've been going out for a few months.'

'What's it like to date a minister? Does he want to kiss and everything?'

'He wants to kiss; I don't know about "everything". He's got hormones, same as anyone else.' I had to smile at her.

'Oooh, oooh,' said Susu, shaking her head in mock horror. 'Roe, you may not have gotten married, but you've dated more interesting people than any of us ever dated.'

'Like who?'

'That policeman, for one. And that writer. And now a priest. Don't the Episcopalians call 'em priests like Catholics do? And remember, even when you were in high school, you dated . . .'

Now, I knew Susu intended this list to cheer me up, but it had exactly the opposite effect. Like looking at my closetful of bridesmaid dresses. So as soon as I could, I started the parting process. As I was getting into my car, I said as casually as I could, 'Did Little Jim have a football game Wednesday evening? I thought I saw your van parked at the Youth Club field.'

'What time?'

'Oh, I guess it was about five thirty.'

'Let me think. No, no, Wednesday afternoon is Bethany's Girl Scout meeting, and Little Jim has Tae Kwon Do at the same time, so Jimmy has to take him to that while I go with Bethany to Scouts. Jimmy has Wednesday afternoons off anyway – that's the afternoon the store is closed, because it's open on Saturdays. I think the older league had a game scheduled for Wednesday. There are lots of vans like ours.'

'Little Jim's Tae Kwon Do is in that building in the shopping center on Fourth Street?'

'Yes, right by that carpet and linoleum place.'

'Does Jimmy get to stay and watch Little Jim's class?'

'No, the teacher won't let parents stay except for special occasions. He says it distracts the boys, especially the littler ones. But the lessons are just half an hour or forty-five minutes. So Jimmy takes a book and reads in the car, or runs an errand. And it's right before supper, too, at five o'clock, so on Wednesdays I have to have leftovers or run home from Scouts and get something out of the freezer to micro-wave.'

Susu didn't seem to think it was strange I was interested in her family's schedule, something she enjoyed detailing anyway. Like any specialist, she wanted to air her know-ledge.

As I finally took my leave and drove away, I was thinking that if Jimmy Hunter had killed Tonia Lee, he'd done it on a tight time budget. Susu hadn't actually said her husband had eaten with the family on Wednesday night, but she hadn't mentioned it was different from any other Wednesday, either. So I had to decide this was inconclusive. But the odds were a little more in favor of Jimmy Hunter's being innocent. It looked as if Patty Cloud's favorite suspect had been sitting outside the Tae Kwon Do studio with a news-paper or a book, or sitting at the country pine table eating supper, at the time Tonia Lee Greenhouse had been killed.

Chapter Five

There was a blinking light on my answering machine.

The first message was from my mother. 'If you haven't taken anything by Donnie Greenhouse's, you need to do that. I took by a chicken casserole this morning, Franklin Farrell said he was going to take a fruit salad of some kind, and Mark Russell from Russell and Dietrich says his wife is making a broccoli casserole. But no one's made a dessert. I know her mother's church will take a lot of stuff, but if you could make a pie, that would mean that the Realtors had provided a full meal. Okay?'

'Make pie,' I wrote on my notepad. (Despite the fact that I was not a Realtor, and I supposed Eileen or Idella knew how to make a pie – probably Mackie, too, for that matter.)

'This is Martin Bartell,' began the second message. 'I'll see you tonight at your mother's.'

I swear the sound of his voice made something vibrate in me. I had it bad, no doubt about it. It was a helpless feeling, kind of like developing rabies, I figured. Though they had shots now for that, didn't they? I wished I could take a shot and be over this thing with Martin Bartell. Aubrey was sexy, too, and a lot safer; perhaps, despite my doubts, our relationship was viable. With an effort, I dismissed Martin from my thoughts and began to rummage through the freezer to see if I had enough pecans for pecan pie.

Not enough pecans. Not enough coconut for German

chocolate pie. (Yes, pie. I never make the cake.) Not any cream cheese for cheesecake. I turned my search to the cabinets. Ha! There was a can of pumpkin that must have come out of Jane's cupboard. I would make a pumpkin pie. I took off my navy blue sweater and put on my old red apron. After tying back my hair, which tends to fly into batter or get caught in dough, I set to work. After I cleaned up and ate my lunch – granola and yogurt and fruit – the pie was ready to go to Donnie Greenhouse's.

Tonia Lee and Donnie's modest home was surrounded by cars. I recognized Franklin Farrell's Lincoln parked right in front, and several more cars looked familiar, though I am not much of a one for remembering cars. Franklin Farrell's was the only powder blue Lincoln in Lawrenceton, and had been the subject of much comment since he'd bought it.

Donnie Greenhouse was right inside the door. He looked white and stunned and yet somehow – exalted. He took my hand, the one that wasn't balancing the pie, and pressed it with both of his.

'You are so kind to come, Roe,' he said with doleful pleasure. 'Please sign the guest book.'

Donnie had been handsome when Tonia Lee had married him seventeen years before. I remembered when they'd eloped; it had been the talk of the town, the high-school-graduation-night elopement that had been 'so romantic' to Tonia Lee's foolish mother and 'goddamned stupid' to Donnie's more realistic father, the high school football coach. Tonia Lee seemed to have worn Donnie thin. He'd been a husky football player when they'd married; now he was bony and looked undernourished in every way. Tonia Lee's horrible death had given Donnie a stature he'd lacked for a long time, but it was not an attractive sight. I was glad

to get my hand back, murmur the correct words of con-
dolence, and escape to put the pie in the kitchen, which was
already full of more homemade food than Donnie had eaten
in the past six months, I'd have been willing to bet.

The cramped little kitchen, which had probably been
ideal for Tonia Lee, a minimalist cook, was full of Tonia's
mom's church buddies, who seemed to be mostly large
ladies in polyester dresses. I looked in vain for Mrs Purdy
herself and asked a couple of the ladies, who suggested I try
the bathroom.

This seemed a bit odd, but I made my way through the
crowd to the hall bathroom. Sure enough, the door was
open and Helen Purdy was seated on the (closed) toilet,
dissolved in tears, with a couple of ladies comforting her.

'Mrs Purdy?' I said tentatively.

'Oh, come in, Roe,' said the stouter of the two atten-
dants, whom I now recognized as Lillian Schmidt, my
former co-worker at the library. 'Helen has cried so hard
she's gotten herself pretty sick, so just in case, we came in
here.'

Oh, great. I made my face stick to its sympathetic lines
and nervously approached Helen Purdy.

'You saw her,' Helen said pitifully, her plain face soggy
with grief. 'How did she look, Aurora?'

A vision of Tonia Lee's obscenely bare bosom flashed
through my head. 'She looked very' – I paused for inspira-
tion – 'peaceful.' The bulging eyes of the dead woman,
staring blankly out from her posed body, looked at me again.
'At rest,' I said, and nodded emphatically to Helen Purdy.

'I hope she went to Jesus,' wailed Helen, and began
crying again.

'I hope so, too,' I whispered from my heart, ignoring the wave of doubt that washed unbidden through my mind.

'She never could find peace on earth, maybe she can find it in heaven.'

Then Helen just seemed to faint, and I backed hastily out of the little bathroom so Lillian and her companion could work over her.

I saw one of the local doctor's nurses in the family room and told her quietly that Helen had collapsed. She hurried to the bathroom, and feeling that I'd done the best I could, I looked around for someone to talk to. I couldn't leave yet – I hadn't been there quite long enough, my inner social clock told me.

I spied Franklin Farrell's head of thick gray hair over the heads crowding the room, and 'excuse me'd' over to him. Franklin, a spectacularly tan and handsome man, had been selling real estate since coming to Lawrenceton thirty or more years before.

'Roe Teagarden,' Franklin said as I reached his side, giving every appearance of great pleasure. 'I'm glad to see you, even though I'm sorry it's here, on such a sad occasion.'

'I'm sorry it's here, too,' I said grimly. I told him about Helen.

He shook his handsome head. 'She has always been wrapped up in Tonia Lee,' he said. 'Tonia Lee was Helen's only child, you know.'

'And Donnie's only wife.'

He looked taken aback. 'Well, yes, but as we all know . . .' Here he realized that bringing up Tonia Lee's infidelities would hardly be proper.

'I know.'

'I brought a fruit salad with Jezebel sauce,' he said, to change the subject. Franklin was one of the few single men in town who didn't mind confessing that he cooked for himself and did it well. His home was also definitely decorated, and beautifully so. Despite his flair for interior design, and his penchant for cooking something other than barbecue, no one had ever accused Franklin of being effeminate. Too many well-known cars had been parked overnight in the vicinity of his house.

'I brought a pumpkin pie.'

'Terry's bringing marinated mushrooms.'

I tried not to gape. It was hard to picture Donnie and Helen Purdy appreciating marinated mushrooms.

'Terry doesn't always have a solid sense of occasion,' Franklin said, enjoying my expression.

Franklin and Terry Sternholtz were certainly the odd pair of the Lawrenceton realty community. Franklin was sophisticated, smooth, a charmer. Everything about him was planned, immaculate, controlled, genial. And here Terry came, covered dish in her hand, her chin-length red hair permed and tossed into fashionable disarray. Terry Sternholtz said just about anything that entered her head, and since she was well-read, an amazing number of things did. She nodded at her boss, grinned at me, and mouthed 'Let me get this to the kitchen' before being swallowed by the crowd. Terry had freckles and an open, all-American face.

In sharp contrast, I found myself staring at a picture of Tonia Lee that hung over the fireplace. It had been taken at one of those instant-glamour photography places that dot suburban malls. Tonia was elaborately made-up, her hair sexily tousled and softer than her normal teased style.

She had a black feather boa trailing across her neck, and her dark eyes were smoldering. It was quite a production, and to have hung it over her fireplace where she could view it constantly meant Tonia Lee had been very pleased with it.

'She was quite a woman,' Franklin said, following my gaze. 'Couldn't sell real estate worth a damn, but she was determined her personal life was going to be memorable.'

That was a strange but appropriate epitaph for the misguided and horribly dead Tonia Lee Greenhouse, née Purdy.

'You go out running every evening right after work, don't you?' I asked him.

'Yes, almost always, unless it's raining or below freezing,' Franklin said agreeably. 'Why?'

'So you must have been out Wednesday evening.'

'I guess so. Yes, it hasn't rained this week, so I must have run.'

'Did you see Mackie Knight?'

He thought. 'So often I see the same people who exercise at the same time I do, and I'm not sure if I did see Mackie that evening or not. I don't always, because I vary my route. There are two I like, and I pretty much alternate them. Mackie seems to pick his at random. I remember it was Wednesday when I saw Terry and Eileen; they walk together most evenings. But I remember only because Terry congratulated me again on a sale I'd made that day. I saw Donnie, riding his bike, that new ten-speed . . . I'm sorry, Roe, I just can't remember about Mackie specifically. How come?'

I told him about Mackie's questioning by the police.

'I can't believe they're so sure another car wasn't there!' Franklin looked very skeptical. 'Someone must have shut their eyes for a minute or two, either the woman across the street or the couple behind the Anderton house. And it seems pretty strange to me that both doors were watched that very night.'

I shrugged. But I thought of what the killer had had to do – move Tonia Lee's car to the rear of Greenhouse Realty, then get home on foot. If the killer's car had been at the house, too, he'd either have had to go all the way back to the Anderton house from Greenhouse Realty to move his own car, or return from taking his own car home to get Tonia Lee's. It seemed almost certain someone would have noticed the other car.

I was thinking of the killer as 'he' because of Tonia Lee's nudity.

Terry Sternholtz returned while I was still thinking it through.

'You look awful grim, Roe,' she said.

'Considering the occasion . . .'

'Sure, sure. It's terrible what happened to Tonia Lee. All us females are going to have to be more careful – right, Eileen?' Eileen had just appeared at Terry's elbow, looking especially impressive in a black-and-white suit and huge black earrings.

'I'm glad we took that self-defense course,' Eileen said.

'When was this?' I asked.

'Oh, a year ago, I guess. We drove into Atlanta to take it. And we practice the moves the woman taught us. But I guess, if Tonia let herself be tied up like that, she wouldn't have had a chance anyway.' Terry shook her head.

Franklin looked startled. He must not have heard that titillating fact. Even worse, Donnie Greenhouse was standing very close, with his back to us, talking to a woman

71

whose hair and glasses were exactly the same gray-blue. But Donnie didn't turn around, so apparently he hadn't heard Terry. She, too, had spotted Donnie and was making a horrified face at us to show she realized her gaffe. Eileen gave her the reproving look you give a close friend, the one that says, 'You blockhead, you did it again, but I love you anyway.'

Eileen and Terry were apparently closer than I'd realized. Now that I considered it, I believed it was Terry who'd answered the phone at Eileen's when I'd called this morning. Eileen was at least ten or more years older than Terry, but they had a lot in common, it seemed. They worked for competing real estate firms, but they were the only single female real estate dealers in Lawrenceton. Well, there was Idella, but she hadn't been divorced very long.

I'd always assumed (along with everyone else in Lawrenceton) that Terry and Franklin were lovers, at least occasionally, because with Franklin's reputation it was impossible to believe he could share an office with a woman and not try to seduce her, and it was assumed in Lawrenceton (especially by the male population) that almost all of his seduction attempts were successful. But the way Franklin and Terry were standing, the way they spoke to each other, didn't add up to an intimate relationship. If I'd had to pick a pair of lovers out of our little group, it would have been Eileen and Terry.

This was an idea I had to adjust to. I had no problem with it. I just had to adjust.

Donnie Greenhouse joined our little circle, and my attention was claimed by his doleful face and his strangely exultant eyes. Somewhere behind those pale compressed lips lurked a grin of triumph. I realized I would rather mash the pumpkin pie in his face than have him eat it, and stomped the thought down into my 'Examine Later' compartment. That compartment was filling up rapidly today. Donnie put his hand on Franklin's shoulder.

'Thanks so much for coming,' the new widower said. 'It's great to know our – my – fellow professionals are showing such support.'

Embarrassed, we all mumbled appropriate things.

'Tonia Lee would have been so pleased to see you all here. Mrs Queensland was here this morning, and Mark Russell and Jamie Dietrich were here, and I see Idella coming in the door . . . this has meant so much to me and Tonia Lee's mom. She's had to lie down in the guest bedroom.'

'Do you have any idea yet when the funeral will be?' Eileen asked.

'Not for sure . . . probably next week sometime. I should be able to get Tonia Lee's – remains back from the autopsy by then. Now, Terry – you be sure and come to the funeral.'

Terry looked considerably surprised. 'Of course I will, Donnie.'

We were all shuffling around trying to figure out what to say when Donnie suddenly burst out, 'I know you all will back me up with the police and tell them I couldn't have hurt Tonia Lee! That woman detective seems to think I could have killed Tonia, but let me tell you' – suddenly he was breathing very fast and other people were turning to look at us – 'if I'd been going to do it, I'd have done it long before this!'

Now *that* I could believe.

The room hushed, and everyone tried to find somewhere else to look. As if moved by one impulse, we all gazed at the ridiculous glamour photograph blown up to such huge proportions above the fireplace. Tonia Lee's false smoldering eyes stared back at us. Her widower broke out in sobs.

This was undoubtedly a scene that would be forever enshrined in Lawrenceton folklore, but telling about it in a year would be a lot more fun than being here at the actual moment it occurred. We all looked at the front door longingly, and as soon as decently possible, the crowd began to flow out, washing the little cluster of Realtors with it. Donnie had pulled himself together enough to shake the hands of those leaving.

I noticed quite a number of them managed to wipe their hands against their clothes, unobtrusively.

I know I did.

An hour of reading the newest Joan Hess restored me. I may have dozed off a little, because when I looked at the clock, I found it was past time to get ready for Mother's dinner party. I dashed up the stairs, took a very brief shower to freshen up, and stood in front of my open closet, faced with a sartorial dilemma. I had to look nice for Aubrey without having it seem as if I was looking my best for Martin Bartell. Well, that was treading a very fine line indeed. What would I have worn if I'd never met Martin? If I were just going to a dinner to greet a new person in town?

I'd wear my royal blue dress and matching pumps, with my pearl earrings. Too dressy? Maybe I should wear nice pants and a pretty blouse? I called my mother to find out what she was wearing. A dress, she told me definitely. But the royal blue suddenly looked boring – high-necked and vaguely military with its two rows of buttons up the front. Then I caught myself thinking of Martin, and I resolutely pulled the blue dress over my head. My hair crackled as I brushed it back and secured the top part over to one side with a fancy barrette. I popped in the pearl earrings, dabbed on a very little scent, and worked on my makeup until the doorbell rang. Before I went down to let Aubrey in, I examined myself in the full-length mirror I'd inherited from Jane. For the thousandth time, I regretted my inability to wear contact lenses, which I'd finally gotten around to trying the previous month. A corner of my mouth turned down. There I was, short, chesty, with round dark brown eyes and so much wavy hair. And round tortoiseshell glasses, and short plain nails with messy cuticles.

It came to me that in my life anything was still possible, but that time might be coming to a close.

Aubrey was clerical that evening – all in black, with his reverse collar. And he looked wonderful that way. He'd seen my dress before, but he still complimented me.

'That's your color,' he said, kissing me on the forehead. 'You ready? You know how I am about dinners at your mother's. Did she hire Mrs Esther?'

'Yes, Aubrey,' I answered with a mocking air of long-suffering. 'Let me get my coat, and we'll go tend to your appetite.'

'It's really cold,' he warned me.

I kept my coats in a downstairs closet. I looked at them for a second before pulling out the new black one. It was beautifully cut, with a high collar. I handed it to Aubrey, who liked to do things like help me on with my coat, even though in my thirty years I'd had plenty of experience. I slid my arms in while he held it, and then he tenderly gathered my hair and pulled it out of the coat and spread it on my shoulders. That was the part he enjoyed. He bent to kiss my ear, and I gave him a sidelong smile.

'Have you seen your new parishioner lately?' I asked.

'Emily, with the little girl?'

There was, something a little different in his voice. I knew it.

'Yes. She was in the office yesterday. She's thinking about buying the house I inherited from Jane.'

I'd discovered Aubrey was interested in me the very day I found out Jane had left me her home and her money and a secret, one I'd never told Aubrey . . . or anyone else. Aubrey had always felt a little uncomfortable about Jane's legacy, since his sensitive cleric's antennae told him people had talked mightily about that strange bequest.

'It's a pretty little house. That would be a good place to raise a child.'

Aubrey had that child on the brain. He hadn't had any with his wife, who had died of cancer.

'I didn't know you were fond of children, Aubrey,' I said very carefully.

'Roe, there's never a good time to talk about this, so I'll talk to you about it now.'

I swung around to face him. My hand had actually been on the doorknob. I know I must have looked alarmed.

'I can't have children.'

He could see from my expression that I was struggling for a response.

'When my wife began to get sick, before we found out what was wrong, we'd been trying, and I went in for tests before her. I found out I was sterile . . . and we found out she had cancer.'

I closed my eyes and leaned against the door for a second.

Then I stepped over to Aubrey and put my arms around him and leaned my head against his chest. 'Oh, honey,' I said softly, 'I'm so sorry.' I stroked his back with one hand.

'Does it make a difference to you?' he asked me softly.

I didn't raise my head. 'I don't know,' I said sadly. 'But I think it makes a difference to you.' I turned up my face then, and he kissed me. Despite Aubrey's principles, we came very close to falling over the edge then and there, at the end of our relationship. There was more emotion in back of our touching than there ever had been before.

'We'd better go,' I said.

'Yes,' he said regretfully.

We were silent all the way to my mother's house on Plantation Drive. We were both a little sad, I think.

Chapter Six

Martin's Mercedes was already parked in front of my mother's house. I took a deep breath and exhaled it into the nippy air as I swung my legs out of the front seat of Aubrey's car. He extended his hand and helped me out, and we went up the long flight of steps to the front door still holding hands. The glass storm door showed us the fireplace, lit and welcoming, and my mother's new husband, John Queensland, standing in front of it with a glass of wine. He saw us coming and held the door for us.

'Come in, come in, it's cold out tonight! I think winter is just about really here,' John said genially. I realized that he now felt at home in the house, he was the host. I, therefore, must be a guest.

This evening was beginning on several jarring notes.

My mother swept in from the kitchen. She could sweep even in quite narrow dresses; you'd think lots of material would be required for that gesture, but not with Aida Teagarden Queensland.

'Aubrey! Aurora! Come get warm and have a glass of wine with our guests,' Mother said, giving me a peck on the cheek and patting Aubrey's shoulder.

He was sitting on the couch, his back to me. I had a little time to get myself steeled. I held Aubrey's hand tighter. We went around the corner of the couch to enter the little 'conversation group' before the fire.

'Have you gotten over your shock of yesterday?' asked Barby Lampton. She was wearing an unbecoming dress in dark green and mustard.

'Yes,' I said briefly. 'And you?'

Aubrey was sliding my coat off. He smoothed my hair gently before he handed the coat to John to hang up. My eyes finally met Martin Bartell's. His face was quite expressionless. His eyes were hot.

'I guess so,' Barby said with a little laugh. 'Nothing like that has ever happened to me before, but a woman I met at the local library this morning was telling me *you've* had an exciting life.'

'Were you taking out a library card?' I asked after a moment.

'Oh, no,' Barby said, letting out a little shriek of laughter. 'I wanted to look at the *New York Times*, at the sale ads. I was thinking about flying up to New York before I go home.'

Her marriage must have left her pretty affluent.

'You're going back so soon?' John asked hastily. Aubrey and I sat on one of the love seats flanking the couch, and Aubrey took my hand again.

'I'm sorry. I must not be cut out for rural living,' Barby said rather smugly. 'This is such a sweet little town, all the people are so – talkative.' And her eyes cut toward me. 'But I miss Chicago more than I thought I would. I'll have to go back and start apartment-hunting. I think Martin was hoping I'd keep house for him, but I don't think I'm quite ready for that.' She smirked at us significantly.

'I understand you got hurt quite badly a couple of years ago?' Barby went on, oblivious to the fact that my mother's back got very straight and even John looked rather grim.

Martin's eyes were going from one face to another curiously.

'Not seriously,' I said finally. 'My collarbone was broken, and two ribs.'

Aubrey was looking studiously at his wineglass. My brush with death had always seemed a little lurid to him.

'Oh, my God! I know that hurt!'

'Yes. It hurt.'

'How did it happen?'

My side began to ache, as it always did when I thought about that horrible night. I heard myself screaming and felt the pain all over again.

'It's old news,' I said.

Barby opened her mouth again.

'I hear you have a wonderful cook, Aida,' Martin said clearly and smoothly.

Barby looked at him in surprise, Mother in gratitude.

'Yes,' she agreed instantly, 'but Mrs Esther is not my cook, really. She's a local caterer. If she knows you well, she'll come into your home and cook for you. If she doesn't know you well, she'll prepare it all and leave it in your kitchen with instructions. Fortunately for me, she knows me well. She picks her own menu, and the next day everyone gets to talk about what Mrs Esther felt like cooking for Mrs Queensland, or Mr Bartell, or whomever. We've all tried to figure out how she selects her dishes, but no one can pick out a pattern.'

Mrs Esther's cooking and character had provided more conversational fodder for parties than any other topic in Lawrenceton. Martin segued smoothly from Mrs Esther to catering disasters at parties he'd attended, Aubrey ran that into bizarre weddings at which he'd officiated, and we were all laughing by the time Mrs Esther appeared in the doorway in a spotless white uniform to announce that it was time to come to the table. She was a tall, heavy black woman with hair always arranged in braids crowning her head, and thick gold hoops in her ears. Mrs Esther – no one ever called her Lucinda – was a serious woman. If she had a sense of humor, she kept it a secret from her clients. Mr Esther was a secret, too. Young Esthers were always on the honor roll printed in the newspaper, and they were apparently as closemouthed as their mother.

We all went into Mother's dining room with a sense of anticipation. Sometimes Mrs Esther cooked French, sometimes traditional Southern, once or twice even German or Creole. Most often it was just American food well prepared and served. Tonight we had baked ham, sweet potato casserole, green beans with small new potatoes, homemade rolls, Waldorf salad, and Hummingbird Cake for dessert. Mother had placed herself and John on the ends, of course, and Aubrey and I faced Barby and Martin, respectively.

I looked at Martin when I thought he was unfolding his napkin. He instantly looked up, and we stared at each other, his hand frozen in the act of shaking out the napkin.

Oh, dear, this was just awful. I would have given anything to be miles and miles away, but there was no excuse I could make to leave just then. I looked away, addressed some remark at random to Aubrey, and resolutely kept my eyes turned down for at least sixty seconds afterward.

Mrs Esther did not serve, though she did remain to clean up afterward. So we were all busy passing dishes and butter for a few minutes. Then Mother asked Aubrey to say grace, and he did with sincerity. I poked at the food on my plate, unable for a few minutes to enjoy it. I stole a quick glance across the table. He was freshly shaved; I bet he'd needed to, he was probably a hairy man. His hair must have been black before it turned white early, his eyebrows were still so dark and striking. His chin was rounded, and his lips curved generously. I wanted Martin Bartell so much it made me sick. It was a dangerous feeling. I had always been wary of dangerous feelings.

I turned to Aubrey, who had chosen this evening of all evenings to tell me about his sterility. To tell me how lovely Emily Kaye's little girl was. To warn me that he wanted children and couldn't have them with me, but that Emily already had a child who could be his in all but name. I had always theoretically wanted a baby of my own, but – I thought now – if I loved Aubrey enough, I would have forgone my own children. If he had loved me enough.

This was not going to happen. Aubrey was not going to hold me fast to his anchor while the danger of Martin Bartell passed by. He was going to cast me adrift, I thought melodramatically. I took a bite of my roll. Martin looked at me, and I smiled. It was better than smoldering at him. He smiled back, and I realized this was the first time I'd seen him look happy. My mother eyed us, and I took another bite of roll.

An hour later we were all protesting how full we were and that the cake had been the clincher. Chairs were pushed back, everyone stood up, my mother swept into the kitchen to compliment Mrs Esther, Barby excused herself, and I walked back into the living room. Martin fell in beside me. Behind us Aubrey and John discussed golf.

'Tomorrow night,' Martin said quietly. 'Let's eat dinner in Atlanta tomorrow night.'

'Just us?' I didn't mean to sound stupid, but I didn't want to be surprised when he turned up with his sister.

'Yes, just us. I'll pick you up at seven.' His fingers brushed mine.

After thirty or forty more minutes of polite conversation, the little dinner party broke up.

Aubrey and I went to his car after Martin and Barby had pulled away, and we exclaimed over how cold it was and how soon Thanksgiving seemed, all of a sudden. Talking about the food lasted us until my place, where he courteously got out to walk me to the door. This was where our dates usually ended; Aubrey wasn't taking chances on being swept away by passion. Tonight he kissed me on the cheek instead of the lips. I felt a surge of grief.

'Good night, Aubrey,' I said in a small voice. 'Good bye.'

'Good-bye, sweetheart,' he said with some sadness. He kissed me again and was gone.

I dragged myself up the stairs to the bedroom and undressed, moving slowly with an exhaustion so deep it was like a drug. Once I'd washed my face and pulled on my nightgown, I crawled into bed and was out when my head hit the pillow.

I woke up slowly the next day. It was sunny and cold. The tree on the front lawn of the townhouse row flicked its bare branches at my window. I was house-hunting this afternoon and had a date for the evening: that made it a very crowded day indeed, by my recent (non-working) standards. I pulled on an old pair of jeans and a shirt, some thick socks and sneakers, and made myself a big breakfast: biscuits, sausage, eggs.

Then I had three hours before Eileen picked me up.

83

Rather than wander around restlessly thinking about Martin, I began to clean. Starting with the downstairs, I picked up, scrubbed, dusted, vacuumed. Once the downstairs was done to my satisfaction, I moved to the upstairs. The guest bedroom was full of boxes of things from Jane's I'd decided to keep, and another bedstead was leaning up against the wall; so cleaning wouldn't be of much use. But in my bedroom I really went to town. My sheets got changed, the bed was perfectly made, the bathroom shone with cleanliness, the towels were fresh, and all my makeup was put away in the drawer where it belonged instead of cluttering the top of my vanity table. I even refolded everything in my chest of drawers.

Then I decided to pick out my clothes for the evening, in case I had a lot of houses to look at today and got home late. What did you wear to a presumably fancy restaurant with a worldly older man you had the hots for?

I'd recently discovered a women's clothing place in the city that stocked things just for petites. My purchases there were among my best and most becoming, because my friend Amina's mom's shop, Great Day, just didn't carry that many petites. Now that I had money, I could buy things even when I didn't need them at the moment. I had one dress I'd been saving for something fancy, if only I had the guts to wear it. It was teal and it shone; it was a little above the knee and had a low neckline and was cut exactly along my body. I took it out of the closet and eyed it nervously. It wasn't what I thought of as indecent, but it certainly complemented my figure.

Now came the indecent part. On the same day, I'd bought an amazing black lace bra and a matching garter belt. This was being seriously naughty for me, and I had been very embarrassed at the cash register. With a sense of casting all caution to the winds, I laid out these garments on the bed, along with some sheer black hose and high-heeled black pumps, and hoped I wouldn't disgrace myself by falling over in them. I wasn't at all sure I had enough confidence to wear this ensemble, but the time was now, if ever. I would aim for this, and if my confidence seeped away during the day and I wore more ordinary undergarments, no one would know I'd chickened out but myself.

It was now almost time for Eileen to come, and I walked through the whole townhouse checking it for details. Everything was clean, orderly, and inviting. I only hoped I wouldn't run into Martin today, since I looked my worst right now.

The doorbell rang at one o'clock on the dot, and when I opened it with my purse in hand and coat halfway on, I was relieved to see Eileen wasn't wearing one of her 'Realtor' outfits, but a pair of nice slacks and a blouse, with a bright fuchsia jacket and sneakers.

'Hi, Roe! Ready to start looking?'

'Sure, Eileen. Is the wind blowing?'

'You bet, and colder than a witch's tit.'

At least it wasn't raining or snowing. But by the look of the leaden sky and the way the trees were tossing, it felt as if it would be raining before long.

'You seemed unsure about what you really wanted,' Eileen began when we were buckled up, 'so I just called around and found out what I could show you today, in your size and price range. We have five houses to see.'

'Oh, that's good.'

'Yes, better than I expected at such short notice. The first one's on Rosemary. Here's the sheet on it . . . it has three bedrooms, two baths, a large kitchen and family room, a formal living room, small yard, and is all electric . . .'

The house on Rosemary needed new carpet and a new roof. That was not insurmountable. What struck it off my list was the narrow lot. My neighbors could look right in my bedroom window and shake hands with me, if they should be so inclined. I'd had too many years of townhouse living for that. If I was going to own a house, I wanted privacy.

The next house had four bedrooms, which I liked, and a poky kitchen with no storage room, which I didn't.

The third house, a two-story in a rather run-down part of Lawrenceton, was most attractive. It needed some renovation, but I could pay for that. I loved the master bedroom, and I loved the breakfast area overlooking the backyard. But the house next door had been divided into apartments, and I didn't like the thought of all the in-and-out traffic – there again, I'd had enough.

The fourth house was a possible. It was a smaller house in a very nice area of town, which meant it cost the same as a larger home elsewhere. But it was only ten years old, was in excellent shape, and had a beautifully landscaped, low-maintenance yard and lots of closets. Also a Jacuzzi in the master bath, which I eyed with interest. It was over my price limit, but not too drastically.

By the time we pulled up in front of the fifth house, Eileen and I had learned a lot about each other. Eileen was intelligent, conscientious, made a note to find out the answer to each and every small query I had, tried to stay out of my way as I considered each property, and was in general a really great Realtor. She at least pretended to consider that not knowing exactly what you wanted was normal.

I was trying to overlook things that I could do something

about if I were really interested in the house, and concentrate instead on things that would absolutely knock the
house out of the running. These things could be pretty
nebulous, though, and then I felt obliged to come up with a
concrete reason to give Eileen.

The fifth house was the killer. There was nothing wrong
with it. It was a three-bedroom with a pleasant yard, a small
but adequate kitchen, and the usual number of closets. It
was certainly big enough for one person. If toys were any
evidence, it was not quite big enough for a couple with
several children. It was very similar to its neighbors . . . the
exterior was one of three or four standardly used in this
subdivision. I was sure anyone on the street would have no
trouble finding her way to any particular room or closet in
any house.

'I hate this house,' I said.

Eileen tapped her fingernails absently on the imitation
wooden-block Formica of the kitchen counter. 'What is it
you dislike so much, so I won't waste our time showing you
anything else with that feature?' A reasonable question.

'It's too much like all the other houses on the street. And
everyone else on this street seems to have little children. I
wouldn't feel a part of the neighborhood.'

Eileen was resigning herself to the fact that I wasn't going
to be the easiest sell she'd ever had.

'This is just the first day,' she said philosophically. 'We'll
see more. And it's not like you have a time limit.'

I nodded, and Eileen dropped me back at my place,
thinking out loud the whole time about what she could
line up to show me in the coming week. I listened with half
my attention, the other half wrapped up in my date tonight.
I was trying to keep my mental screen absolutely blank,

trying not to imagine any scenes from the evening, trying not even to conjecture on its outcome.

Of course, I still had time to kill when I got home, and with the house clean and my clothes selected, nothing to kill it with. So I turned on the television, and when that failed, I tried to concentrate on an old Catherine Aird, counting on her never-failing blend of humor and detection to get me through a couple of hours. After ten minutes of concentrated effort, Aird worked, as she always did. I even forgot to look at my watch for minutes at a time.

Then I remembered I hadn't done my exercise video that morning. Madeleine came to watch with her usual amazement, and I worked up quite a sweat and felt very virtuous.

Finally it really was time for a shower.

I hadn't scrubbed myself this much since my senior prom. Every atom of my skin and inch of my hair was absolutely clean, every extra hair was shaved from my legs, and when I emerged I slapped everything on myself I could think of, even cuticle cream on my messy cuticles. I plucked my eyebrows. I put on my makeup with the care and deliberation of a high-fashion model, and dried my hair to the last strand, brushing it afterward at least fifty times. I even cleaned my glasses.

I wiggled into my incredible underwear without looking in the mirror, at least not until I pulled the black slip over my head. Then, very carefully, the teal dress, which I zipped up with some difficulty. I switched purses, put on my high-heeled pumps, and surveyed myself in Jane's mirror.

I looked as good as I possibly could, and if it wasn't good enough . . . so be it.

I went downstairs to wait.

Chapter Seven

The doorbell rang exactly on the dot.

Martin was wearing a gorgeous gray suit. After a moment I stepped back to let him in, and he looked around.

Suddenly we realized we weren't observing the amenities, and both of us burst into speech at once. I blurted 'How've you been doing?' as he said 'Nice apartment.' We both shuddered to a halt and smiled at each other in embarrassment.

'I reserved a table at a restaurant the board of directors took me to after they'd decided to hire me for the job here,' Martin said. 'It's French, and I thought it was very good. Do you like French food?'

I wouldn't understand the menu. 'That'll be fine,' I said. 'You'll have to order for me. I haven't tried to speak French since high school.'

'We'll have to rely on the waiter,' Martin said. 'I speak Spanish and some Vietnamese, but only a little French.'

We had one thing in common.

I got my black coat from the coat closet. I slid it on myself, not being ready for him to touch me. I lifted my hair out of the collar and let it hang down my back, acutely conscious that he watched my every move. I thought if we made it out the door it would be amazing, so I kept my distance; and when he opened the door for me to pass through, I did so as quickly as I could. Then he opened the patio gate and the door of his car. I hadn't felt so frail in years.

His car was wonderful – real leather and an impressive dashboard. It even smelled expensive. I had never ridden in anything so luxurious. I was feeling more pampered by the moment.

We swept imperially through Lawrenceton, attracting (I hoped) lots of attention, and hit the short interstate stretch to Atlanta. Our small talk was extremely small. The air in the car was crackling with tension.

'You've always lived here?'

'Yes. I did go away to college, and I did some graduate work. But then I came back here, and I've been here ever since. Where have you lived?'

'Well. I grew up in rural Ohio, as I mentioned last night,' he said.

I could not picture him being rural at any point in his life, and I said so.

'I've spent my lifetime eradicating it,' he said with some humor. 'I was in the Marines for a while, in Vietnam, the tail end, and then when I came back, after a while I began to work for Pan-Am Agra. I finished college through night school, and Pan-Am Agra needed Spanish speakers so much that I became fluent. It paid off, and I began working my way up . . . this car was the first thing I got that said I had arrived, and I take good care of it.'

Presumably the big house in Lawrenceton would be another acquisition affirming that he was climbing the ladder successfully.

'You're – thirty?' he said suddenly.

'Yes.'

'I'm forty-five. You don't mind?'

'How could I?'

Our eyes moved simultaneously to a lighted motel sign looming over the interstate.

The exit was a mile away.

I thought I was about to give way to an impulse – finally.

'Ah – Aurora—'

'Roe.'

'I don't want you to think I don't want to spend money on you. I don't want you to think I don't want to be seen with you. But tonight . . .'

'Pull off.'

'What?'

'Pull off.'

Off the interstate we rolled at what seemed to me incredible speed, and suddenly we were parked in front of the bright office of the motel. I couldn't remember the name of it, where we were, anything.

Martin left the car abruptly, and I watched him register. He carefully did not turn to look back at me during the interminable process.

Then he slid back into the car with a key in hand.

I turned to him and said through clenched teeth, 'I hope it's on the ground floor.'

It was.

It rained during the night. The lightning flashed through the windows, and I heard the cold spray hit the pavement outside. He had been sleeping; he woke up a little when I shivered at the thunder. 'Safe,' he said, gathering me to him. 'Safe.' He kissed my hair and fell back into sleep.

I wondered if I was. In a practical way I was safe, yes; we

were not stupid people; we took precautions. But in my heart I had no feeling, none at all, of safety.

The morning was not the kind that ordinarily made me cheerful. It was colder, grayer, and puddles of muddy water dotted the parking lot of the motel. But I felt good enough to overcome even the faint sleaziness of putting back on the same clothes I'd worn. We ate breakfast in the motel coffee shop, and both of us were very hungry.

'I don't know what we've started,' Martin said suddenly, as he was about to get up to pay our bill, 'but I want you to know I have never felt so wrung out in my life.'

'Relaxed,' I corrected smilingly. 'I'm relaxed.'

'Then,' he said with raised eyebrows, 'you didn't work hard enough.'

We smiled at each other. 'A matter of opinion,' I said, quite shocked at myself.

'We'll just have to try again until we're both satisfied,' Martin murmured.

'What a fate,' I said.

'Tonight?' he asked.

'Tomorrow night. Give me a chance to recoup.'

'See, you do know some French words,' he replied, and we smiled at each other again. He glanced at his watch as we drove back. 'I'm usually working at the plant alone on Sunday, but today we're having a special meeting at twelve thirty, followed by an executives' lunch. It's a kickoff for our next production phase.'

'What will they say if you're a few minutes late?' I asked him softly when he kissed me good-bye at my townhouse door.

'They won't say anything,' he told me. 'I'm the top dog.'

For the first time in a long time, I was going to skip church. I staggered up the stairs and stripped off all my clothes, pulled a nightgown over my head, and after turning off the bell of the phone, crawled in bed to rest. I began to think, and with an effort turned off the trickle of thought like a hand tightening a faucet. I was sore, exhausted, and intoxicated, and soon I was also asleep.

My mother called at eleven, as soon as she got home from church. The Episcopalians in Lawrenceton had a nine thirty service, because Aubrey went to another, smaller church forty miles away to hold another service directly after the Lawrenceton one. I was drowsing in bed, trying to think of what to do with the remainder of the day, persuading myself not to call Martin. I felt so calm and limp that I thought I might slide out of bed and ooze across the carpet to the closet. I barely heard the downstairs phone ringing.

'Hello, Aurora,' Mother said briskly. 'We missed you at church. What have you been doing today?'

I smiled blissfully at the ceiling and said, 'Nothing in particular.'

'I called to find out about the annual Realtors' banquet,' she said. 'Would you and Aubrey like to come? It's for families, too, you know, and you might enjoy it, since you know everyone.' Mother tried to get me there every year, and the last year I'd broken down and gone. The annual Realtors' banquet was one of those strange events no one can possibly like but everyone must attend. It was a local custom that had begun fifteen years before when a Realtor (who has since left town) decided it would be a good thing if all the town professionals and their guests met once a year and drank a lot of cocktails and ate a heavy meal, and afterward sat in a stupor listening to a speaker.

'Isn't the timing a little bad this year?' I was thinking of Tonia Lee.

'Well, yes, but we've made the reservations and selected the menu and everyone's kept that night free for months. So we might as well go through with it. Shall I put you and Aubrey down? This is the final tally of guests. I'll be glad when Franklin's in charge of this next year.' Each agency in Lawrenceton took the task in turn.

'He'll leave most of the arrangements to Terry Stern-holtz, the same way you left them to Patty,' I said.

'At least it won't be our agency that looks inefficient if anything goes wrong.'

'Nothing's going to go wrong. You know how efficient Patty is.'

'Lord, yes.' My mother sighed. 'I sense you're putting me off, Aurora.'

'Yes, actually I am. I just wanted to sort of tell you something . . .'

' "Sort of"?'

'I'm trying to glide into this.'

'Glide. Quickly.'

'I'm not dating Aubrey anymore.'

An intake of breath from Mother's end.

'I'm really just . . . I think . . . I'm seeing Martin. Bartell.'

Long silence. Finally Mother said, 'Were there any bad feelings, Aurora? Do John and I need to skip church for the next couple of weeks? Aubrey was a little somber today, maybe, but not so much that I thought anything about it until I talked to you.'

'No bad feelings.'

'All right. I'll have to hear the whole story from you sometime.'

'Sure. Yes, well, Martin and I will come, I think . . . maybe.' I had a sudden attack of insecurity. 'It's next Saturday night, right?'

'Right. And Tonia Lee will be buried Tuesday. Donnie called today. The church service is at' – Mother checked her notes – 'Flaming Sword of God Bible Church,' she finished in an arid voice.

'Golly. That's out on the highway, isn't it?'

'Yes, right by Pine Needle Trailer Park.' Mother's voice could have dried out the Sahara.

'What time?'

'Ten o'clock.'

'Okay. I'll be there.'

'Aurora. You're okay? About this change in beaus?'

'Yes. So is Aubrey. So is Martin.'

'All right, then. See you Tuesday morning, if not before. I think Eileen mentioned she had some more properties to show you this afternoon; she should be calling you soon.'

'Okay. See you.'

I took a quick shower, pulled on a green-, rust-, and brown-striped sweater, the matching rust-colored pants, and my brown boots. A glance outside had shown that the day had not brightened, but remained resolutely cold, windy, and wet.

Downstairs I found my answering-machine light was blinking. I'd been too tired to glance that way this morning.

'Roe, this is Eileen, calling on Saturday evening. I have two houses to show you Sunday afternoon if it's convenient for you, in the afternoon. Give me a call.'

A moment of silence between messages.

'Roe, are you asleep?' My face flushed when I heard Martin's voice. He'd probably called while I was in the shower. 'I'm calling from work, sweetheart. I can hardly wait until tomorrow night. I can't make it to Atlanta that night since I have a meeting early Tuesday morning, but we can at least go to the Carriage House.' That being Lawrenceton's best restaurant. 'I want to see you again,' he said simply. 'You made me very happy.'

I was pretty damn happy myself.

I called Eileen back to make an appointment for two o'clock, then decided to treat myself to lunch somewhere. On impulse, I punched the number of my reporter friend, Sally Allison, and we arranged to meet at the local Beef 'N More.

Thirty minutes later we were settled opposite each other, after waiting in line through the Sunday church crowd. Sally was working on a hamburger and a salad, and I had virtuously opted for the salad bar only, though I could certainly get enough calories from what was spread up and down its length.

Sally was older than I by more than twelve years, but we're good friends. She was a Sally who wouldn't tolerate a nickname. Sally had bronze hair, never out of place, and she bought expensive clothes and ran them into the ground. She was wearing a black suit I'd seen on her countless times, and it still looked good. For once, she had some news to impart before she started digging for more.

'Paul's working today. He and I got married last week-end,' she said casually, and the cellophane package of crackers I was trying to open exploded. I hastily began to gather up the crumbs.

'You married your first husband's brother?'

'You know we've been dating for a long time.'

'Well, yes, but I didn't know it was going to result in a marriage!'

'He's great.'

We chatted away. I was dying to know what the first Mr Allison thought of this new situation, but was aware I really must not ask.

The third time Sally was explaining to me how wonderful Paul was (she knew I'd heard while dating Arthur Smith that Paul had never been popular with his fellow detectives), I was sufficiently bored and skeptical to look around me. To my surprise, I spied Donnie Greenhouse eating lunch with Idella. They were sitting in one of the few places in the steak house where you could talk without being overheard. Donnie was leaning over the table, talking earnestly and quickly to Idella, whose delicate coloring was showing unbecoming blotches of stress. Idella was shaking her head from side to side.

What an odd couple! It was a little strange to see Donnie out in public, even though I dismissed that reaction on my part as uncharitable. But with Idella?

'They certainly look put out with each other,' Sally said. She'd followed my gaze. 'I don't think this is a widower on the rebound, do you?'

There sure wasn't anything loverlike in their posture or in the way they were looking at each other. Suddenly Idella sprang up, grabbed her purse, and headed for the women's room. Donnie scowled after her. I thought Idella was crying.

Sally and I exchanged glances.

'I guess I better go check,' I said. 'There's a fine line

between showing concern and butting in, and this situation is right on it.'

The two-stall salmon-and-tan women's room was empty except for Idella. She was indeed crying, shut in one of the booths.

'Idella,' I said gently. 'It's Roe. I'm holding the door shut so no one else can come in.' And I braced my back against the door.

'Thanks,' she sobbed. 'I'll straighten up in a minute.'

And sure enough, she pulled herself together and emerged from the booth, though not until I'd had time to decipher the last batch of graffiti through a layer of tan paint. Showing some wear and tear, Idella ran some cold water on a paper towel and held it over her eyes.

'It's going to ruin my makeup,' she said, 'but at least my eyes won't be so puffy.'

It was oddly difficult to talk to her with her eyes covered like that, in this bleak room with the smell of industrial disinfectant clogging my nostrils.

'Idella, are you all right?'

'Oh . . . yes, I'll be okay.' She didn't sound as though she were certain. 'Donnie just has some crazy idea in his head, and he won't let it go, and he's hounding me about it.'

I waited expectantly. I was so curious I finally prodded her. 'He surely doesn't think you had anything to do with Tonia Lee's death?'

'He thinks I know who did do it,' Idella said wearily. 'That's just ridiculous, of course.' She stared bleakly into the mirror; she looked even more haggard under the harsh light, her dead-grass hair a limp mess around her pale face. 'He says he saw my car pulling out of the Greenhouse Realty parking lot the night Tonia Lee was killed.'

'How could he possibly think that?'

But Idella was through confiding, and when someone pushed behind me hard enough to make the door move a little, she seized the chance to go back to her table. 'Thanks,' she said quickly. 'I'll see you later.'

I moved away from the door to let her out, and she shouldered her way past the door-pusher, who turned out to be Terry Sternholtz.

She gave us a very peculiar look; she knew I'd been holding the door shut. I wondered if she'd been out there long.

'Idella seemed upset,' Terry said casually as she pulled open one of the stalls. She looked very bright today, her bouncing red hair contrasting cheerfully with a kelly green suit.

'Some upset she had,' I said dismissively, and went back to my table. Sally was waiting, and raised her eyebrows expectantly as I slid into my chair.

'I don't know,' I said to answer Sally's unspoken query. 'She wouldn't really say.' I didn't want to repeat the conversation. It seemed evident Idella was in trouble of some kind, and she had always been so nice to me I didn't want to compound it by starting a rumor. Sally looked at me sideways, to show me she knew I was evading her. 'I don't know why you think I tell everyone everything I know,' she said with more than a little pique in her voice. It looked as if we'd have our own little quarrel.

Just then the group of Pan-Am Agra executives came in for their campaign kick-off lunch, among them Martin. It was just like seeing the boy who'd given you your first kiss the night before. As if I'd had on a homing signal, Martin immediately turned and scanned the crowd, finding me quickly. He excused himself from his companions and left the line to come over. My face felt hot. Sally's back was to him, and she was saying 'You look like you just swallowed a fish, Roe,' when he came up, bent over, and gave me a kiss that was just short enough not to be vulgar. Then we beamed at each other.

'This is my friend Sally Allison, Martin,' I said abruptly, suddenly aware of Sally's interested face.

'Hello,' he said politely, and shook Sally's proferred hand.

'Aren't you the new plant manager of Pan-Am Agra?' she asked. 'I think Jack Forrest did a business-page article on you.'

'I saw it. It was well written,' Martin said. 'More than I can say for some of the stories written about me. What time tomorrow night, Roe?'

'Seven?' I said at random.

'I'll be there at seven.' He kissed me again very quickly, nodded to Sally, and rejoined his group, who were watching with great attention.

'You certainly got branded in public,' Sally said dryly.

'Huh?' I had my face turned down to my plate.

' "Property of Martin Bartell. Do Not Touch".'

'Sally, I don't want to look like we're talking about him,' I hissed. I looked at her sternly. 'Just talk about something else for a while.'

'Okay,' she said agreeably. 'Is he going to ask you to the prom?'

'Sally!'

'Oh, all right. Donnie left in a snit as soon as Idella emerged from the women's room and hot-footed it out the door. Donnie looked right sullen. What did she tell you?'

'That Donnie thought . . . oh, Sally!'

'Just curious, just curious! Since when are you and Martin Bartell an item?'

'Very recently.' Like last night.

'Well, isn't life on the up-and-up for us? I get married, and you get a sweetie.'

I rolled my eyes. Thinking of Martin as a 'sweetie' was like thinking of a Great Dane as a precious bundle of fur.

'He was in Vietnam, wasn't he?' Sally asked.

'Yes.'

'I think he brought home some medals. He wouldn't talk about it to Jack, but one of the other Pan-Am Agra execs told Jack that Bartell came out of the war with a bit of glory.'

'When was the story in the paper?' I hadn't seen it.

'Soon after he arrived, at least six weeks ago.'

'Can you send me a copy, Sally?'

'Sure. I'll track it down when I go to the office to-morrow.'

We computed tips and gathered our purses. My shoulder blades itched, and I looked behind me. Martin, surrounded by his employees, was sitting at one of the larger round tables, watching me, smiling a little.

He looked hungry.

I floated out to my car.

Chapter Eight

I had agreed to meet Eileen at the office, and it was close enough to the time for me to head that way. There were several cars parked outside; Sunday was often a busy day at Select Realty.

The first person I saw was Idella, who said 'Hi, Roe!' as brightly as if I hadn't seen her boo-hooing in the women's room at a restaurant not forty-five minutes before.

'Hello, Idella,' I said obligingly.

'I just got an offer on your house on Honor. Mrs Kaye is offering three thousand less than your asking price, plus she wants the microwave and the appliances to stay.'

We went to Idella's little office, decorated exclusively with pictures of her two children, together and separate, the boy about ten and very heavyset, the girl perhaps seven and thin, with lank blond hair. I sat in one of her client chairs and considered for a moment.

'Tell her – her offer needs to be up by a thousand, and she can have everything but the washer and dryer.' Mine came with the townhouse, and I'd need a set when I moved.

'What about the freezer in the carport toolshed?' Idella asked. 'It's not spelled out here whether she is including that under appliances or not.'

'I don't really care that much about the freezer. If she wants it, she can have it.'

'Okay. I'll take your counteroffer over to her aunt's house right now.'

Idella was obviously determined not to refer to the scene at Beef 'N More. Of course, I wanted to know what it was about, but in all decency I would have to wait until she felt like confiding in me.

'I'm really pleased about this offer,' I told her, and she smiled.

'It was an easy sell, the right person at the right time,' she said dismissively. 'She needs a small decent house in good shape, you have a small decent house in good shape; the dead-end street location and the price are right.'

The phone rang while Idella gathered papers. She picked up with one hand while her other kept busy. 'Idella Yates speaking,' she said pleasantly. The first words of her caller changed Idella's demeanor dramatically. Her free hand stilled, she sat up straighter, the smile vanished from her face. 'I'll have to talk later,' she said swiftly. 'Yes, I have to see you . . . well . . .' She closed her eyes in thought. 'Okay,' she said finally. She hung up and sat very still for a moment. The cheer, the bustle, had seeped right out of her. I didn't know whether to say anything or not, so I settled for looking concerned, as I certainly was.

Idella decided to stonewall. 'I think I've got everything here,' she said in a dreadful simulation of her previous cheerful efficiency.

'If you need help, you know you can count on me and my mother,' I told her, and left her office for Eileen's.

Just as Eileen got up to go, she received an unexpected call from an out-of-town client who'd decided to make an offer on a house he'd seen the week before. The house was listed with Today's Homes, but the client had been referred to Eileen personally, so she had shown it along with a lot of Select Realty listings. It took Eileen some time to hammer out the client's offer, assure the client that she'd call Today's Homes that very second, then hang up and immediately lift the phone to dial. I had fished my book out of my purse several minutes before and was reading contentedly.

'Franklin? Eileen. Listen, that Mr and Mrs McCann I showed the Nordstrom house to last week, they just called . . . Yep, they want to make an offer . . . I know, I know, but here it is . . .' As Eileen relayed the offer to Franklin, I became immersed in my book. I was almost through with the Catherine Aird.

Finally Eileen was ready to set out. I told her the good news about the probable sale of my own house as we got into her car.

'Does Idella seem okay to you?' I asked cautiously.

'Lately, no.'

'I think something's wrong.'

'What? Anything we can do something about?'

'Well – no.'

'If we don't know, and she doesn't ask for help, seems like we aren't wanted,' Eileen said, giving me a straight look.

I nodded glumly.

At the first house, the owners were on their way out as we pulled up to the curb. Eileen had cleared the showing with them first, of course, and she went up to talk to them while I surveyed the yard, which badly needed raking.

'How are the two of you?' Eileen said in her booming voice. 'Ben, you ready to go out with me yet?'

'The minute Leda lets me off the rope,' the man

answered with equally heavy good humor. 'You better get out your dancing shoes.'

'Haven't you found Mr Right yet, Eileen?' the woman asked.

'No, honey, I still haven't found anyone who's man enough for me!'

They chuckled their way through some more faintly bawdy dialogue, and then the couple pulled off in their car while Eileen unlocked the front door.

'What?' Eileen said sharply.

I hadn't known anything was showing on my face.

'Why do you do that, Eileen?' I asked as neutrally as I could. 'Is that really you?'

'No, of course not,' she said crisply. 'But how many houses am I going to sell in this small town if Terry and I go out in public holding hands, Roe? How would we make a living here? It's a bit easier for Terry in some ways . . . Franklin actually wanted someone working for him who was immune to his charm. He didn't want to fall into bedding an employee. But still, if everyone knew . . . and the people who do know have to be able to pretend not to.'

I could see her point, though it was depressing.

'So here is the Mays' house,' Eileen said, resuming her Realtor's mantle with a warning rattle. 'We have – three bedrooms, two baths, a family room, a small formal living room . . . mmmm . . . a walk-in closet off the master bedroom . . .'

And we strolled through the Mays' house, which was dark and gloomy, even in the kitchen. I could tell within two minutes I would never buy this house, but this seemed to be a day for pretense. I was pretending I might, Eileen was pretending the preceding conversation hadn't taken place. Idella had been pretending she wasn't upset by the phone call in her office.

My lack of sleep began to catch up with me by the hall bathroom, which I viewed dutifully, opening the linen closet and yawning into it, noting the hideous towels the Mays had wisely put away.

'Are you with me today, Roe?'

'What? Oh, I'm sorry, I didn't sleep too well last night.'

'Do you even want to go see this other house?'

'Yes, I promise I'll pay attention. I just don't like this one, Eileen.'

'Just say so. There's no point in our spending time in a house you don't want.'

I nodded obediently.

We were short on conversation and long on silence as we drove to our next destination. Lost in daydreams, I barely noticed when Eileen began to leave town.

Just a mile east out of Lawrenceton, we came to a house almost in the middle of a field. It had a long gravel drive-way. It was a two-storey brick house, and the brick had been painted white to set off the green shutters and a green front door. There was a screened-in porch. The second storey was smaller than the first. There was a separate, wide two-car garage to the left rear, with a covered walk from a door in the side of the garage to the house. There was a second storey to the garage, with a flight of stairs also covered, leading up to it.

The sun was beginning to set over the fields. It was much later than I'd thought.

'Eileen,' I said in amazement, 'isn't this—'

'The Julius house,' she finished.

'It's for sale?'

'Has been for years.'

'And you're showing it to me?'

She smiled. 'You might like it.'

I took a deep breath and got out of the car. The fields around the house were bare for the winter, and the yard was bleached and dead. The huge evergreen bushes that lined the property were still deep green, and the holly around the foundation needed trimming.

'The heirs have kept it going all this time,' I said in amazement.

'Just one heir. Mrs Julius's mother. She wanted to turn the electricity off, of course, but the house would just have rotted. There's been surprisingly little vandalism, for the reputation it has.'

'Well. Let's go in.'

This was turning out to be an unexpectedly interesting day. Eileen led the way, keys in hand, up the four front steps with their wrought-iron railing painted black, badly needing a touch-up now. We went in the screen door and crossed the porch to the front door.

'How old is it, Eileen?'

'Forty years,' she said. 'At least. But before the Juliuses disappeared, they had the whole house rewired . . . they had a new roof put on . . . a new furnace installed. That was . . . let me check the sheet . . . yes, six years ago.'

'And they had the extra storey put on the garage?'

'Yes, it was a mother-in-law apartment. Mrs Julius's mother lived there. But of course you remember.'

The disappearance of the Julius family had been the sensation of the decade in Lawrenceton. Though they had some family in town, few other people had had a chance to get to know them, so almost everyone had been able to enjoy the unmitigated thrill of the mystery and drama of their vanishing. T. C. and Hope Julius, both in their early forties, and Charity Julius, fifteen, had been gone when Mrs Julius's mother came over for breakfast, as was her invariable habit, one Saturday morning. After calling for a while, the older woman had searched through the house. After she'd waited uneasily for an hour, and finally checked to see that their vehicles were still there, she'd called the police. Who of course had at first been skeptical.

But as the day progressed, and the family car and pickup truck remained parked in the garage, and no member of the Julius family called or returned, the police became as uneasy as Mrs Julius's mother. The family hadn't gone bike riding, or hiking, hadn't accepted an invitation from another family.

They never came back, and no one ever found them.

Eileen pushed open the front door, and I stepped in.

I don't know what I'd expected, but there was nothing eerie about the house. The cold sunshine poured through the windows, and instead of sensing ghostly presences of the unfound Julius family, I felt peace.

'There's one bedroom downstairs,' Eileen read, 'and two upstairs, plus a room up there used for an office or a sewing room . . . of course, that could be a bedroom, too. And there's an attic, with a boarded floor. Very small. Access through a trapdoor in the upstairs hall.'

We were in the family room, a large room with many windows. The pale carpet smelled mildewy. The double doors into the dining room were glass-paned. The dining room had a wood floor and a built-in hutch and a big window with a view of the side yard and the garage. After that came the kitchen, which had an eat-in area and many,

many cabinets. Lots of counter space. The linoleum was a sort of burnished orange, and the wallpaper was cream with a tiny pattern of the same color. The kitchen curtains were cream with a ruffle of the burnished orange. There was a walk-in pantry that had apparently been converted into a washer-dryer closet.

I loved it.

The downstairs bathroom needed work. New tile, recaulking, a new mirror.

The downstairs bedroom would make a great library.

The stairs were steep but not terrifying. The banister seemed quite solid.

The largest bedroom upstairs was very nice. I didn't like the wallpaper too much, but that was easily changed. Again, the upstairs bath, which opened into the hall, needed some work. The other bedroom needed painting. The small room, usable as a storeroom or sewing room, also needed painting.

I could do that. Or better yet, I could have it done.

'You look pretty happy,' Eileen observed.

I had forgotten anyone else was there.

'You are actually considering buying this house,' she said slowly.

'It's a wonderful house,' I said in a daze.

'A little isolated.'

'Quiet.'

'A little desolate.'

'Peaceful.'

'Hmmm. Well, as far as price goes, it's a bargain . . . and of course, there's the little apartment over the garage that you can rent to whomever . . . that'll help with the isolation, too.'

'Let's see the apartment.'

So down the stairs and out the kitchen door we trooped. The flight of stairs up to the little second floor seemed sturdy enough; of course, this addition was only six years old. I followed Eileen up, and she unlocked the glass-paned door.

It was really one large open area, the only sealed-off part being a bathroom at one end. The bathroom had a shower, no tub. The kitchen was just enough for one person to heat up a few things from time to time; the mother had gone over to the house for most of her meals. Some nice open shelves had been built in, and there were two closets. There was a window air conditioner, but no hint of how it had been heated.

'A kerosene space heater is my guess,' Eileen said. 'There shouldn't be any problem in an area this size.'

Perhaps I could rent this to a student at Lawrenceton's little Bible college or to a single schoolteacher. Someone quiet and respectable.

'I really like this,' I told Eileen unnecessarily.

'I can tell.'

'But I need to think about it, of course.'

'Of course.'

'I can afford it, and the repairs, and pay for it outright. But it is stuck out of town, and I need to decide if that would make me nervous. On the other hand, I can practically see Mother's house from here. And if you could find out who owns this field, I'd appreciate it. I wouldn't want to buy out here and then discover someone was putting up a discount mall. Or a chicken farm.'

Eileen scribbled a note to herself.

I told myself silently that if any of these variables didn't work out, I would hire an architect and have a house very similar to this one built from scratch.

'And I'll keep looking, too,' I told Eileen. 'I just don't want to see anything cramped.'

'Okay, you're the boss,' Eileen said agreeably. It had grown dark enough for her to switch on the car lights as she turned around on the apron to the side of the garage to negotiate the long driveway.

We went back to town in silence, Eileen obviously trying not to give me some good advice, I in deep thought. *I really liked that house.*

'Wait a minute,' Eileen said, her voice sharp.

I snapped out of my reverie.

'Look, that's Idella's car. But she's not showing the Westley house today. My God, look at the time! I'm showing it in an hour to a couple who work different shifts all week. I'm going to need that key.'

Eileen was seriously miffed. If I'd been just any client, she would have waited until she got me back to the office and then returned to or called the listing, but since I was part of the Realtor family, she felt free to vent in front of me. Eileen pulled into the driveway and swung out of her car with practiced ease. I got out, too. Maybe Idella would know if Emily Kaye had already responded to my counteroffer.

There was no client car parked by Idella's.

'The Westleys moved last week,' Eileen said, and opened the front door without knocking. 'Idella!' she hooted. 'I'm going to need this key in an hour, woman!'

Nothing. All within was dark. We went in slowly.

For once, Eileen seemed disconcerted.

Eileen called again, but with less expectation that she would be answered. The blinds and curtains were all open, letting in some light from the streetlamp one lot away.

Eileen tried to flip on a light, but the electricity had been turned off.

The house was very cold, and I pulled my coat tighter around me.

'We should leave and call the police,' I said finally.

'What if she's hurt?'

'Oh, Eileen! You know . . .' I couldn't finish the sentence. 'All right,' I said, bowing to the inevitable. 'Do you have a flashlight in your car?'

'Yes, I do. I don't know where my head is!' Eileen exclaimed, thoroughly angry with herself. She fetched the flashlight and swept its broad beam around the family room. Nothing but dust on the carpet. I followed her and her flashlight into the kitchen . . . nothing there. So, back past the front door and down the hall to the bedrooms. Nothing in the first one to the left. Nothing in the bathroom. By now, tears were running down Eileen's face and I could actually hear her teeth chattering.

Nothing in the second bedroom.

Nothing in the hall linen closet.

Idella was in the last bedroom. The flashlight caught her pale hair, and the beam reluctantly went back to her and stayed.

She was crumpled in a corner like a discarded bedspread. Tonia Lee had been arranged, but Idella had just been dumped. No living person could have been lying that way.

I made myself step forward and touch Idella's wrist. It was faintly warm. There was no pulse. I held my hand in front of her nostrils. No breath. I touched the base of her thin neck. Nothing.

You never know about people. I heard a slithery sound,

and the flashlight beam played wildly over the walls as tough Eileen Norris slid to the floor in a dead faint.

Of course, there wasn't a phone in the Westley house. I had the sudden feeling I was on an island in the middle of a populous stream. I hated to leave Eileen alone in the dark and silence with Idella's corpse, but I had to get help. There was a car at the house to the right of the Westleys', the helpful flashlight revealed, and I knocked on the screen door.

A toddler answered, in a red-checked shirt and overalls. I couldn't tell if it was a little boy or a little girl. 'Could I speak to your mommy?' I said. The child nodded and left, and after a moment a young woman with a towel around her hair came to the door.

'I'm sorry, I've told Jeffrey not to answer the door, but if I don't hear the doorbell in time, he zooms to it,' she said, making it clear she thought that very clever of Jeffrey. 'Can I help you?'

'I'm Aurora Teagarden,' I began, and her face twitched before the polite lines reasserted themselves. 'I need you to call the police for me. There's been a – an accident next door at the Westley house.'

'You're really serious,' she said doubtfully. 'No one should be in that house, it's for sale.'

'I promise you I am serious. Please call the police.'

'All right, I will. Are you okay, yourself?' she asked, terrified I would ask to be let into her home.

'I'm fine. I'll go back over there now if you'll call.' I had the distinct feeling that she would much rather have gone back to washing her hair and forgotten that I'd knocked.

'I'll call right now,' she promised with sudden resolution.

So I went back over to the cold black house next door. Eileen was stirring around but still out of it. I gripped the flashlight defensively as I crouched next to her on the nasty brown carpet, and stared dully at a dead beetle while I waited for the police.

At least Jack Burns didn't show up. I would rather have been in a locked room with a pit bull than have faced Sergeant Burns at that moment. He had regarded me with baleful mistrust ever since we'd come across each other during the Real Murders investigation. He seemed to think I was the Calamity Jane of Lawrenceton, that death followed me like a bad smell. If I'd been Jonah, he'd have thrown me to the whale without a qualm.

Lynn Liggett Smith seemed to take my presence as a matter of course. That was almost as disturbing.

Eileen came out of her faint, we were allowed to tell the little we knew, and then I drove a shaken Eileen back to the office. My mother had already been called by the police, so she had waited there. Eileen went to Mother's office in a wobbly parody of her usual brisk trot. There were lights on down the hall. I slid into the client chair in Mackie Knight's office. With considerable astonishment, Mackie put down the paperwork he was doing.

'What's happening, Roe?'

'Have you been here all afternoon, Mackie? Till now?' I saw by the clock on the office wall that it was already seven.

'No. I just came back after spending all afternoon at church and eating supper at home with my folks. Just as my mom put her lemon meringue pie in front of me, I remembered that I didn't have all the papers ready for the Feiffer closing tomorrow morning.' There was lemon meringue smeared on a Styrofoam plate and a used plastic fork on a corner of his desk.

'Was anyone else at your folks'?'

'Yeah, my minister. What's this about?'

'Idella was just killed.'

'Oh, no.' Mackie looked sick. 'Where?'

'At the empty Westley house.'

'How?'

'I don't know.' I hadn't seen a weapon, but Idella's coat had been covering her throat. The poor light hadn't been reliable, but I'd thought her face had had the same funny tone as Tonia Lee's. 'Maybe strangled.'

'The poor woman. Who's told her kids?'

'I guess the police. Or maybe whoever she left the kids with while she worked.'

'And I couldn't have done it!' Mackie said, the penny finally dropping. 'I've been with someone every blessed minute, except driving time from my folks' back here.'

'Maybe this wasn't planned as well as Tonia Lee's murder.'

'You think Tonia Lee was killed at the time she was killed and the place she was killed because there would be a lot of available suspects.'

'Sure, don't you?'

'I hadn't thought about it that way,' he said slowly, 'but it makes good sense. Poor Idella.' Mackie shook his head in disbelief. 'She sure had been acting funny lately, almost apologetic, every time I talked to her.'

'She knew you didn't kill Tonia Lee, Mackie. I think she knew who did, or suspected.'

We both sat and thought for a while, and then my

mother came to the door and asked gently if she could speak to me for a moment.

'Mackie,' she said as I got up to leave his office, 'you went to church after Idella left the office? Or before?'

'Before. She was still in her office when I walked out the door. I said good-bye to her.'

'Oh, thank God. You're in the clear, then.'

'Yes, I think I am.' Mackie was having a hard time with conflicting emotions.

Lynn was waiting in Mother's office.

'I hear you had an interesting conversation with Idella at Beef 'N More,' she said.

I thought Lynn was bluffing, but I'd intended telling her what Idella had said anyway, vague though it was. The only person who could have told Lynn that I'd talked to Idella at lunch was Sally Allison, and Sally didn't know what Idella had said to me. No, I wasn't being fair to Sally . . . there was Terry Sternholtz.

I told Lynn all about Idella's and my little bathroom tête-à-tête. We went over and over it while my mother listened or worked quietly. I wondered why I was sitting here instead of going down to the police station. I told Lynn, frontward and backward and upside down, every little nuance of Idella's apparent fight with Donnie Greenhouse, her flight to the women's room, my half-hearted attempt to help her, her few comments to me, and her departure from the restaurant. My next glimpse of her at the office, my brief conversation with her here, the exchange with an unknown person she'd had over the telephone, and her statement that she was going to go to Emily Kaye with my counteroffer. Then how I'd found her at the empty house.

By the time Lynn was satisfied she'd gotten everything

out of me she could get, I was heartily sorry I'd spoken to Idella at the restaurant. Sometimes good impulses backfire.

'Go talk to Donnie Greenhouse,' I said irritably. 'He was the one who upset her, not me.'

'Oh, we will,' Lynn assured me. 'In fact, someone's talking to him right now.'

But Donnie Greenhouse, who'd let Tonia Lee stomp on him for so long, would not yield an inch to the police. He called my mother while I was still in her office and told her triumphantly he hadn't given Paul Allison the time of day.

'He told Paul that no matter what Roe Teagarden said Idella told her, he and Idella had discussed nothing more than business and Tonia Lee's funeral.' My mother's famous eyebrows were arched at their most skeptical.

'He might as well wear a sign that says "Please Kill Me. I Know Too Much",' I said.

'Donnie doesn't have enough sense to come in out of the rain, but I didn't think he was this dumb,' Mother said. 'And why he's doing it, instead of telling the police all he knows, I cannot fathom.'

'He wants to avenge Tonia Lee himself?'

'God knows why. Everyone knows she made his life hell on wheels.'

'Maybe he always loved her.' Mother and I pondered that separately.

'I personally don't think a rational person with a sense of self-preservation could continue to love under such a stream of abuse as that,' my mother said.

I wondered if she was right. 'So Donnie's not rational and has no sense of self-preservation,' I said. 'And what about Idella? Evidently the call she got in her office was from someone she suspected might be the killer. And yet she apparently agreed to meet this person in an empty house. Doesn't that sound like she loved whoever it was?'

'I just don't love that way,' said Mother finally. 'I loved your father until he was unfaithful.' This was the first time she'd ever said one word to me about her marriage with my father. 'I loved him, in my opinion, very deeply. But when he hurt me so much, and things weren't going well otherwise, it just killed the love. How can you keep on loving when someone lies to you?' She really could not understand it.

I didn't know, with my limited experience, if my mother just had an extraordinarily strong sense of self-preservation, or if the world was full of irrational people.

'It seems from what I've read, and observed,' I said hesitantly, 'that lots of people aren't that way. They keep on loving, no matter what the hurt or cost.'

'No self-respect. That's what I believe,' my mother said crisply. She stared out her window for a moment, at the bare branches of the oak tree outside, which made a bleak abstract pattern against the gray sky. 'Poor Idella,' she said, and a tear oozed down her cheek. 'She was worth ten Tonia Lees, and she had children. She'd done so much for herself since her husband left her. I'd gotten pretty fond of her without ever getting really close to her.' Mother looked back at me. Our eyes met. 'She must have been so frightened.' Then she shook herself. 'I'll have Eileen call Emily Kaye to find out if Idella'd actually gotten over there with your counteroffer, honey. The police should let us have the papers in her car, soon. We can get on with the house sale, with Eileen or me taking Idella's part. I'll let you know.'

I hadn't been worried about it at all. 'Thanks,' I said,

trying to look relieved. 'I think I'll go home now.' But I turned at her office door to say, 'You know, I'll bet money that Donnie doesn't really know anything at all. If he does get killed, it'll be over absolutely nothing.'

I was really glad I hadn't agreed to meet Martin tonight. I needed a little time to get over this horror. Driving home, I felt the impulse to call him nonetheless. But I shook my head. No telling what he was doing. Still trying to inspire Pan-Am Agra executives, eating supper with a client, working in his motel room on important papers. I hated him to find out how lonely I was, so soon.

I kept thinking about Idella, her children, her death from love.

Chapter Nine

The next morning my best friend, Amina Day – now Amina Day Price – called me. I'd just pulled on my blue jeans, and I lay across the bed on my stomach to grab the phone.

'Hi, it's me!'

'Amina,' I said happily, feeling my mouth break into a smile, 'how are you?'

'Honey, I'm pregnant!'

'Ohmigod!'

'Yes! Really, really. The ring in the tube turned the right color this morning, and I lost my breakfast, too. So I'm home lying down.'

'Amina, I can't believe it. What does Hugh say?'

'He's just thrilled. He's ready to go out now and buy a car seat and a crib. I told him he better wait a while, my mother always told me it was bad luck to start getting ready too soon.'

'Have you seen a doctor?'

'No, I have an appointment for next week with the obstetrician all the wives of Hugh's partners go to.'

Hugh is an up-and-coming lawyer in Houston.

'I'm so glad for you,' I told her honestly.

We talked for a while. Or, rather, I listened while Amina talked to me about the baby and what she wanted and didn't want for this exceptional infant.

'So what's new with you?' she asked finally.

'Well . . . I'm seeing someone.'

'Not the minister?'

'No, not anymore. This man – Martin – he's the new plant manager at Pan-Am Agra.'

'Wo-wo. How old is he?'

'Older.'

'Rich?'

'Well-to-do.'

'Of course, that doesn't make any difference anymore, since you inherited all that loot.'

'No, but it's nice anyway. He likes having money.'

'Tell me all!'

'Well, his name is Martin Bartell, he's forty-five, he has white hair but his eyebrows are black . . .'

'Sexy!'

'Yes, very . . . he's tough, strong, intelligent, and . . . ruthless. You wouldn't want to try to bullshit him.'

'These are not Boy Scout attributes.'

'You know, you're right,' I said thoughtfully. 'He's definitely not a Boy Scout type. More of a street fighter.'

'I hope he's not too tough for you.'

'No matter what he is,' I confessed, 'this is the worst I've ever had it. I'm scared to death. I couldn't stay away from him if he were on fire.'

'Oh, wow. You do have it bad. I hope he's worthy of this. This sounds like a "love at first sight" thing.'

'Yes, the first time I've ever experienced it. And, I hope, the last. It's awful.'

'I've never had it like that,' Amina said. 'So what else is happening?' It wasn't like Amina to change the subject. Could she be a bit envious?

But I filled her in on Tonia Lee's murder and the resultant

confusion. Then I told her about Susu Hunter's husband and his strange secret persona as the House Hunter.

'Oh, I'm like that to a lesser extent,' Amina said instantly. 'It's not so weird.'

'You just like to look at houses?'

'Sure, don't you? I get a tingle at the base of my spine when I walk into a house that's not mine, that I can look at all I want. It's like stepping into someone else's life for a while. You can open the closets, and find out what they pay for electricity, and how many clothes they have, and how clean their furniture is . . . I have had the best time since Hugh and I started looking for a house. I wish I could look at houses all the time. In fact, I thought about becoming a Realtor instead of a legal secretary until I realized I'd have to get out in all kinds of weather and deal with jerks who didn't know what they wanted . . . you know.'

'That's interesting, Amina,' I said, and meant it.

'Of course, now we're looking at *bigger* houses,' she added, and we were back on her favorite topic of the moment.

By the time we hung up, I'd agreed to be the baby's godmother and Amina had urged me to hurry and marry Martin if we were going to anyway, so she could be a matron of honor before her stomach got too big.

I just laughed and said good-bye. It made me nervous to think of marriage and Martin in the same sentence, as if it were a jinx. I finished dressing, trying not to feel sorry for myself, only glad for Amina and Hugh.

I found myself wondering if Jimmy Hunter had been Idella's lover. It would make perfect sense, given his house-hunting aberration, for him to pick a Realtor as a lover. But how would that tie in with the things missing from houses listed with local Realtors? Surely Jimmy hadn't been lifting them while he toured the houses? He just couldn't have, not without a Realtor noticing. And it wasn't always Idella who'd shown him around. Hadn't someone at the meeting at Select Realty said the Greenhouses had always made sure Tonia Lee escorted him? Had something in Tonia Lee's sharp nature punctured the balloon of Jimmy's fantasy life as a house hunter, something so upsetting he'd killed her for it?

Jimmy Hunter drove a blue Ford Escort, and so had Idella. Maybe it had been Jimmy's car Donnie Greenhouse had seen Wednesday night. Come to think of it, what had Donnie been doing out himself? It must have been after the presumed time of Tonia Lee's death, which must have taken place before the neighbors to the rear of the Anderton place had noticed her car had gone. About the time of Tonia Lee's death, Jimmy had been parked outside the Tae Kwon Doe studio waiting for his son.

I shook my head at myself while I peered in the mirror applying my makeup. I was just getting confused. I wasn't going to speculate about depressing things anymore. I was going shopping to buy a dress to wear tonight. I was going to find out if Emily Kaye had accepted my counteroffer on the house on Honor. It would be nice and tidy to have that little chapter of my life closed, Jane's house settled and all my things ready to put into a home I owned. And I thought of the Julius house again: the sun through the windows, the warm kitchen, the porch.

'You'd like it,' I told Madeleine, who was squinting at me doubtfully in the one pool of sunshine in my bedroom. She rolled on her back to invite me to tickle her stomach, and I obliged. We went downstairs together to change her water and fill her food bowl.

I called Mother's office before I set out for my petite dress shop in Atlanta. Eileen said that the police had given her the contract for my house, signed by Emily Kaye. It had been in Idella's car. The changes I had stipulated had been penciled in, and Emily herself had called that morning after she heard the news of Idella's death, to confirm that she had agreed to the price and to my wanting the washer and dryer. So on my way out of town, I stopped by the office and signed the contract, too. And Jane's house was on its way to becoming Emily Kaye's house, having never really been my house at all.

I was willing to drive all the way into the city instead of going to Great Day, Amina's mom's store, because I wanted something that Amina called a 'Later, Baby' dress. Amina had always been a dating specialist, one who picked her clothes with as much care as she picked her makeup. Your clothes always said something to your date, she claimed, and she had had such a long and varied and successful dating career that I figured she knew what she was talking about.

'It has to be modest enough to where you could see your mom while you were in it without turning red,' she had advised. 'But it has to kind of growl to your date, "Later, baby!"'

It was a slow day at the petite shop, Short 'n Sweet (hey, I didn't name it), and the saleswoman who'd helped me before was glad to see me. I was too embarrassed to spell out what I wanted, but I tracked it down eventually. It was a sweater dress, soft and beige and shapeless but clingy, with a big cowl collar – and you wore it almost off the shoulders.

I had to buy a strapless bra to go under it, and then big gold earrings, and then some shoes, so I made the saleswoman's afternoon a happy one. Quite a switch for someone who had worn her college and high school clothes for ten years.

I ate lunch in the city and visited my favorite bookstore, so I came home to Lawrenceton fairly laden down with good things.

I tuned in to the local radio station as I left the interstate. It was time for the news. 'Police are questioning a suspect in the murder of a Lawrenceton Realtor,' said the newswoman chattily. 'Today a prominent local businessman was taken in for questioning regarding the death of Tonia Lee Greenhouse, who was found strangled in an empty home last week. Though police would not comment, an unnamed source says police will also question James Hunter in connection with the death of Idella Yates, whose body was found yesterday.'

I sucked in my breath. Jimmy Hunter. Poor Susu! Poor kids! I wondered what new evidence Lynn had uncovered that had led to Jimmy's being taken to the police station. I thought perhaps the police had found some of the stolen things in Jimmy's possession. Or maybe . . . but it was no use speculating.

Martin was ten minutes early.

He took in the dress appreciatively.

'I just have to brush my hair,' I said, my hands extended to hold him off.

'Let me,' he suggested, and I could feel a blush that began at my toes.

'We'll never get there if I do,' I said with a smile, and scampered up the stairs before he could grab me.

'One kiss,' he said as I came back down minutes later. He and Madeleine had been regarding one another warily.

'One,' I said strictly.

It was very sweet at first, but then it began to steam up.

'My glasses are fogging,' I murmured.

He laughed. 'Okay, we'll go.'

But it wasn't until a few minutes later that we got into his car. It didn't take long to get to the Carriage House, which had actually formerly been what its name implied. It was the only fancy restaurant in Lawrenceton, and had very good food and service. It was small, dark, and expensive, with a large added-on room at the back where local groups held dinners. We were shown a corner table and sat side by side on the L-shaped banquette.

Being so close to Martin was seriously interfering with my paying attention to anything else, but I was determined to get through a normal-date evening with him. We talked about what wine to order, and I selected my food; and he talked to the waiter, and the wine arrived.

'Jimmy Hunter's being questioned about the death of the woman whose body we found,' I told him.

'I heard someone was. Do you know the man?'

So I told Martin about Jimmy and Susu, and Jimmy's little quirk.

'He likes to look at houses with female Realtors? That's pretty – kinky.'

'But he's never done anything to anybody,' I pointed out fairly. 'And frankly, I hope the police have got something more on him than that, as I assume they must, because I find it very hard to believe that Jimmy did it.' I hadn't known I felt that way until it came out of my mouth. 'And they haven't charged him in Tonia Lee's murder, or Idella's, and surely the same person killed them both.'

But Martin hadn't heard about my finding Idella's body, and I had to tell him now, his light brown eyes fixed on my face.

'I wish you had called me when you were upset,' he said. I had an uneasy feeling that he might be a little angry with me.

'I thought about you. Of course. It's just that – really – for all our emotions for each other, we really don't know each other that well. And you're the plant manager, you have all kinds of duties and responsibilities that I don't know anything about, Martin. Even on Sunday night, I just felt very hesitant about interrupting you.'

I had been able to picture all too clearly his exasperated face as he turned away from some important papers to answer a call from his one-night flame.

'Listen,' he said intently. 'Don't. We haven't learned a lot about each other, but this is not just a bed thing. I hope. On my part, anyway, and I think for you, too.'

I didn't know, yet.

He touched my hair. 'If you need me, I'll come. That's all there is to it. We have time to get to know each other. But if anything bothers you or upsets you, you call me.'

'Okay,' I said finally, with misgivings.

Our salads arrived and we began eating, very conscious of each other.

'Martin, you'll have to tell me about your company,' I said. 'I have only the vaguest idea of what Pan-Am Agra does.'

'We arrange for the exchange of good used farm machinery for the produce from some of the South American countries,' he explained. 'Also, we manufacture some agricultural goods and food using raw materials from North and South America, which is what we do at the plant here. And we own land in South America where we're trying to use North American farming methods to produce better yields. Those are the main things Pan-Am Agra does, though there are a few other things, too.'

'What kind of products does Pan-Am Agra make?'

'Some fruit blends, some products containing coffee, some fertilizer.'

'Do you have to travel to South America much?'

'When I was at company headquarters in Chicago, I had to go often, at least once every month. Now I won't fly down as much. But I will have to visit the other plants.'

'Is the government very much involved in what you do?'

'As a regulatory agency, yes, too much so. They're forever thinking we're smuggling drugs in or weapons out, knowingly or unknowingly, and our shipments are almost always searched.'

I thought of searching fertilizer, or the raw materials thereof, and wrinkled my nose.

'Exactly,' Martin said.

'So what is a pirate like you doing in an agricultural company?'

'Is that the way you see me? A pirate?' He laughed. 'What is a quiet, slightly shy, introverted librarian doing dating a pirate like me? Your life has changed a lot lately, if what you tell me and what other people tell me is true.'

I noticed he hadn't answered my question.

'My life has changed a lot,' I said thoughtfully. 'I'm changing with it, I guess.' Funny, I'd never thought of myself changing, just my circumstances. 'I guess it started

– oh, almost two years ago,' I told him, 'when Mamie Wright was killed the night it was my turn to address Real Murders.'

The salads left, and the main course came while I was telling Martin about Real Murders and what had happened that spring.

'You're certainly not going to think I'm quiet after hearing all that,' I said ruefully. 'You had better tell me about your growing up, Martin.'

'I don't like to think about it much,' he said after a moment. 'My father died in a farm accident when I was six . . . a tractor overturned. My mother remarried when I was ten. He was a hard man. Still is. He didn't put up with any nonsense, and he had a broad definition of nonsense. I didn't mind him at first. But I couldn't stand him after a few years.'

'What about your mom?'

'She was great,' he said instantly, with the warmest smile I'd seen. 'You could tell her just about anything. She cooked all the time, did things you just see mothers in old sitcoms doing now. She wore aprons, and she went to church, and she came to every game I played – baseball, basketball, football. She did the same for Barbara.'

'You said you grew up in a small town, too?'

'Yes. A few miles outside the town, actually. So I wasn't sorry to get the chance at this job here, I wanted to see what it would be like to be back in a small town again, though Lawrenceton is really on the edge of Atlanta.'

'Your mother isn't alive anymore?'

'No, Mom died when I was in high school. She had a brain aneurysm, and it happened very – very suddenly. My stepfather is still alive, still on the farm, but I haven't seen him since I came home from the war. Barbara goes back to town every now and then, just to show off how far beyond that little place she is now, I think . . . she doesn't see him, either.'

'There was a rift?'

'He won't sell the farm.'

I didn't think that answered my question.

'Mother left the farm to him for his lifetime, and left us a little cash. Of course, she didn't have much. But we're supposed to get a third of the proceeds if he ever sells it, or if he dies before selling it, we get the land. We wanted him to sell when she died so we could move into town. But he wouldn't sell, out of some damn stubbornness. Now the situation for small farms is even worse, as I'm sure you're aware.' I nodded soberly. 'So the farm's falling down, the barn has a hole in the roof, he hasn't made money in years, and the whole thing is rotting. He could sell anytime to our nearest neighbor, but out of sheer meanness he won't.' Martin stabbed his steak with his fork.

We ate for a minute in silence. I thought over what he'd said.

'Um – how many times have you been married?' I asked apprehensively.

'Once.'

'Divorced?'

'Yes. We had been married for ten years . . . we had a son, Barrett. He's twenty-three now . . . he wants to be an actor.'

'A chancy profession.' I thought of my mystery-writer friend, Robin Crusoe, now in California writing a television movie script based on his latest book, and wondered how he was making out.

'That's what I told him. Funny thing – he already knew it!' Martin said wryly. 'But he wanted so much to try, I gave him the money to get started. If he doesn't make it, he at least needs to know he gave it his best shot.'

'You sound as though you didn't get the encouragement you needed at some point.'

He looked surprised for a moment. 'I guess that's right. Though it's hard to say what I really wanted to do. I don't know that I ever formulated it. Something big,' and his hands made a circle in the air. We laughed. 'It had to be something I could leave my hometown for.'

'I've never wanted to leave my hometown,' I said.

'Would you?'

'I've never had a reason to. I don't know.' I tried to remember what it had been like when I went to college: not knowing anyone, not knowing where anything was, the first two weeks of uncertainty.

The waiter came up at that moment to see if we needed anything. 'Will you be wanting any dessert tonight?'

Martin turned questioningly to me. I shook my head.

'No,' he told the waiter. 'We'll have ours later.' He smiled at me, and I felt a quiver that went down to my shoes.

Martin paid the bill, and I realized I hadn't said a word about it being my turn. Something about Martin discouraged such offers. We would have to talk about that.

But not right away.

We were quite ready for dessert when we got to my place.

Chapter Ten

'Martin,' I said later in the night, 'can you go with me to the Realtors' banquet Saturday night?'

'Sure,' he said sleepily. He wound a strand of my hair around his finger. 'Do you ever wear it up?' he asked.

'Oh, sometimes.' I rolled over so it hung around his face like a curtain.

'Could you wear it up Saturday night?'

'I guess so,' I said warily.

'I love your ears,' he said, and demonstrated that he did.

'In *that* case,' I said, 'I will.'

A thud on the foot of the bed made Martin jump.

'It's Madeleine,' I said hastily.

I could feel him relax all over. 'I have to get used to the cat?'

'Yes, I'm afraid so. She's old,' I said consolingly. 'Well, actually, middle-aged.'

'Like me, huh?'

'Oh, yes, you practically have one foot in the grave,' I said.

'Ooo – do that again.'

So I did.

'I have to go out of town late this afternoon,' Martin said over toast early the next morning. He had stowed some extra clothes and shaving gear in his car, so he was ready for work.

'Where to?' I tried not to feel dismayed. This relationship was so new and perilous and fragile, and I was so constantly afraid Martin did not feel what I felt, so often aware of the differences in our ages, experiences, goals.

'Back to Chicago, to report on the plant reorganization to the higher-ups. I've been cutting out a lot of deadwood, finding out the weak points in the plant management. That's what I was brought in to do.'

'Not a popular job.'

'No. I've made some people mad,' he said matter-of-factly. 'But it's going to make the plant more efficient in the long run.'

'How long will you be gone?'

'Just Wednesday and Thursday. I'll fly back in Friday morning. But why don't we have lunch today? Meet me out at the Athletic Club at twelve thirty, and we'll go from there, if that suits your plans.'

'Okay. But please let me take you to lunch this time, my treat.'

The look on his face had to be seen to be believed. I burst into giggles.

'You know, that's the first time a woman ever offered to take me out,' he said finally. 'Other men have told me it's happened to them. But never to me. A first.' He tried very hard not to glance around at my apartment, so much humbler than any place he'd be used to living in since he'd climbed the business ladder.

'We don't have to go to McDonald's,' I said gently.

'Sweetheart, you don't have a job—'

'Martin, I'm rich.' Gosh, that word still gave me a thrill.

'Maybe not what you would think of as rich, but still I have plenty of money.'

'Inherited?' he asked.

'Uh-huh. From a little old lady who just wanted me to have it.'

'No relation?'

'None.'

'You're just a lucky woman,' Martin said, and proceeded to demonstrate just how lucky I was.

'You'll mess up your suit,' I said after a moment.

'Damn the suit.'

'You told me you have an appointment at eight thirty.'

He released me reluctantly.

'See you later,' he said.

I gave him a light kiss on the cheek. 'Twelve thirty,' I said.

I had an unpleasant task to face that morning. I had decided I should go see Susu. All the people who wrote in to 'Ann Landers' and 'Dear Abby' complained that they felt neglected when someone in the family had serious legal problems or went to jail, that people tried to act as if it hadn't happened or stayed away entirely. While Jimmy hadn't exactly been arrested, I didn't want to be a fair-weather friend to Susu, though time and circumstance had certainly created a gulf between us. So I pulled on a bright sweater and black pants, and red boots to go with the sweater. Cheerful, casual – as if it were an everyday catastrophe that had befallen the Hunter family.

It took me a second to recognize Susu when she came to the door. Her veneer was stripped away, and so much of Susu depended on that veneer. Her shoulders sagged, her eyes were red-rimmed, her clothes were – it seemed – deliberately shabby and old. She looked as if she'd reached back in her closet for the things she was saving to pull on when she painted the carport. There were dirty dishes piled up in the sink. Susu was not only genuinely a woman in the midst of a crisis, she was also acting out the part.

'Where are the kids?' I asked cautiously.

'I sent them to my sister in Atlanta.' As if she'd put them in a box and taken them down to the post office.

'You're here all by yourself?'

'Not a soul has come by except our minister.'

'What's the story on Jimmy?'

'He's down at our lawyer's office right now. They kept him all day yesterday. I think they may arrest him today.'

'Susu, you think he did it!'

'What else can I think?'

'Well, *I* don't think he did it.'

'You don't?' She sounded amazed.

'Susu! Of course not!'

'His fingerprints were in the Anderton house.'

'So? Hasn't it occurred to you there are several ways they could have gotten there without him having been the one to kill Tonia Lee?'

'Like how, Roe? Just tell me how!'

'Maybe some other Realtor showed him over the house. Maybe Tonia Lee did show him the house, and then he left and her date showed up and killed her!'

'Jimmy must have been having an affair with her, Roe. Then she threatened to tell me or the kids and he killed her. He must have just lost his temper.'

'I could kick you in the rear, Susu Hunter. You are making up things you can't possibly know. You get yourself into that shower upstairs and get your nice clothes on and put on your makeup and go down to your lawyer's office and you *ask him yourself.*'

I was probably doing exactly the wrong thing. Susu would get down there and Jimmy would say, 'Yeah, I did it. And I had been having an affair with her, too.'

Saint Aurora, I told myself sardonically.

But Susu was actually doing it. She went up the stairs at a pace a little brisker than her previous shamble. She was patting her hair absently, doing some damage-control evaluation.

I washed the dishes. I left them in the drainer to irritate Susu into putting them away.

She came down in thirty minutes, looking more like herself.

'When is he supposed to have done her in?' I asked.

'Well, Wednesday night.'

'But he took your son to karate practice, or something, that evening, didn't he? And he was at work until then, right? After practice, he came right home to supper?'

'Yes.'

So much for it having been Jimmy's car Donnie had seen.

'So when did he find time to go over to the Anderton house, screw Tonia Lee, and kill her?' I asked.

'That's true,' she said slowly. 'I guess I was just so quick to believe he did it because he's been acting so funny lately.'

'He may be going through a hard time, Susu. He may even need therapy or something. But I really don't think Jimmy ever killed anyone.'

'I'd better get down there. Thanks for coming by, Roe. I just kind of gave up.'

'Sure,' I said, not feeling noble at all.

'Of course, if he did do it, I'll never want to see you again,' she said with a tiny smile.

'I know.'

She'd never been as dumb as she liked to seem.

I was getting back into my car when suddenly I realized that this was the morning of Tonia's funeral. *Another* unpleasant task. I looked at my watch. I had thirty minutes. I raced back to the townhouse, dashed up the stairs, tore off my clothes and pulled on my winter black dress, loose and long with a drop waist. No time to bother with a slip; no time to pull on panty hose. I rummaged through the closet and got my black boots. The dress needed a necklace or scarf or something, but there simply wasn't time, and my earrings would just have to do. I yanked on my coat and ran to the car.

The Flaming Sword of God Bible Church was a rectangular cement-block building painted white, with a parking lot of ruts and dust. A cold wind whistled straight through my clothes as I got out of my car. I pulled my coat tighter around me with one hand and held my hair out of my face with the other. I gusted into the little church along with the chilly wind. The parking area had been crowded, and the church was jammed to capacity. I'd seen a television news truck outside, parked in the rear along with the hearse, and the camera crew was in the church. I was willing to bet Donnie was responsible for that. There was no place to sit; every pew was jam-packed with solid Lawrencetonians in their winter coats. I hovered at the back, trying to spot a dark corner. My mother's basilisk glare found me anyway. Of course, she'd arrived on time, and was seated decorously in the middle of the church, along with the other members of the staff of Select Realty. They were all there except Debbie Lincoln, who presumably was manning the phone at the office.

For a moment I looked for Idella, before I remembered.

The coffin was sitting at the front of the church. I was thankful it was closed. It was covered with a pall of red carnations, and the sharp scent of the flowers carried through the chilly air. There was no organ, but a pianist was playing something subdued and doleful, maybe 'Nearer, My God, to Thee'. The minister entered from a door by the altar. He was a plain young acne-scarred man, with eyebrows and lashes so light they were almost invisible. He clutched a Bible, and he had on a cheap dark suit, white shirt, and black tie. There was a shifting on all the hard pews. I recognized Mrs Purdy down at the front, wearing navy blue and pearls. Beside her, Donnie's white face stood out over a suit of unrelieved black.

'Let us bow our heads in prayer,' the minister intoned. His voice was unexpectedly rich. I did so, uneasily aware that a member of the camera crew was eyeing me with speculation. I began to edge away as unobtrusively as possible. I was afraid I had been recognized. The cameras had caught me before, when the Real Murders deaths had taken place. Surely no one would approach me until the service was over. The cameraman had poked the reporter, a very young woman I recognized faintly from the very few times she'd been on the air. He was whispering in her ear, and she was staring in my direction. My name had not been in the newspaper accounts of Tonia Lee's death, thank God, at least as far as I knew.

I had a hard time concentrating on the sermon, which from the snatches I caught seemed to be a combination of

'She is at peace now, whatever her life and last moments were like' and 'We must forgive the erring human who has strayed so far from God . . . Vengeance is mine, saith the Lord'. The congregation seemed to meet this last idea with some resistance at first, but by the time the minister ended, heads were nodding in agreement. I hadn't caught the man's name, but this preacher seemed to be a man of some persuasion.

The whole thing seemed to go by quickly, what with one thing and another. The pallbearers assembled and began to carry out the coffin, with some head-nods and murmurs among them to coordinate the lifting. Everyone rose, and the piano began to mourn again. For the last time, Tonia Lee left a house of the living. The camera crew became busy filming this, and I managed to work my way down the line of pews until I was even with the one where the Select Realty crowd was situated. After allowing enough time for the coffin to be loaded into the hearse, which I'd heard pulling around to the front door, the minister gave a closing prayer, doleful and fervent, and the congregation began to file out to their cars. All I had to do was whisper to Mother that the cameraman had recognized me, and the Select Realty staff closed around me. I managed to get to Mother's car thus camouflaged, and squeezed in with Mother, Eileen, Patty, and Mackie, who had stood out in the Flaming Sword of God Bible Church like a chocolate drop on a wedding cake.

I hadn't planned on going to the cemetery, but it seemed as though I had to.

None of us talked much on the ride to Shady Rest. I was thinking of how soon we'd be doing this again, whenever Idella was buried. Eileen was still washed out and subdued from our experience Sunday. Mackie was always quiet in a social setting, at least in one involving whites. For all I knew, he sang solo in the choir at the African Methodist Episcopal church.

Mother was grim about the news crew. Patty was upset by the funeral itself. 'I've never been to one before,' she explained, and I wondered if she'd only come to this one because my mother had assumed she would.

I looked around the crowd at the gravesite. Under the green tent, in the front row of folding chairs, sat Mrs Purdy and Donnie and a thin-lipped woman I recognized as Donnie's older sister. Tonia Lee's aunt and cousins sat behind them.

The chilly wind whipped among the mourners, making the tent awning flap and the red pall ripple. It brought tears to eyes that otherwise wouldn't have shed any. Franklin Farrell, his gray hair for once ruffled, was standing at the back of the crowd, looking a little bored. Sally Allison was there in a neat dark gray suit, her tan eyes flickering over the assemblage. Lillian, my former co-worker, had ended up with her face to the wind and was blinking furiously and shivering. Lynn Liggett Smith, muffled in a heavy brown coat, was scanning the crowd with sharp eyes.

At least the graveside service was short. It helped that Donnie had decided to play the dignified widower rather than opting for histrionics. He contented himself with throwing a single red rose on the coffin. Mrs Purdy burst into sobs at this romantic gesture, and had to be consoled with patting and hugging during the remainder of the service. I thought perhaps she was the only person there who genuinely regretted the ending of Tonia Lee's life.

On our subdued ride back to the church, where Mother

dropped me off by my car, I found myself wondering how Susu and Jimmy were getting along.

I looked at my watch. It was almost time to meet Martin. I looked dreadful. Standing still in the cold had drained all color from my face, and my hair had been whipped around until it looked like a long dust mop. In the rearview mirror, I looked at least five years over my age. I pulled some lipstick out of my purse and put it on. I did have a brush, so I tried to tame my hair. I was marginally more presentable when I got through.

The Athletic Club was a fairly new enterprise in Lawrenceton. Built only a couple of years before, it offered memberships to businesses and individuals. It featured weight rooms, exercise classes, and racquet-ball courts, plus a sauna and whirlpool. My mother took aerobics classes there. I explained to the dismayingly fit woman at the front desk – she was wearing orange-and-pink-striped spandex and had her hair in a ponytail – that I was meeting Martin Bartell, and she told me he was still playing racquetball on the second court. 'You can watch if you climb those stairs,' she said helpfully, pointing to the easily visible stairs five feet to her left.

Sure enough, one side of the second-floor hall was faced with Plexiglas that overlooked the racquetball courts. The other side had ordinary doors in an ordinary wall, and from behind one of them I could hear shouted instructions ('Okay! Now BEND!') to an exercise class, backed by the deep-bass beat of rock music. The first racquetball court was empty, but in the second court the only sounds were the rebound of bodies and the ball from the walls, and the grunts of impact. Martin was playing killer racquetball with a man about ten years younger than he, and Martin was playing with a single-minded will and determination that gave me pause. In the five or six minutes they played, I learned a lot about Martin. He was ruthless, as I'd sensed. He was a man who could push the edge of fair play, staying just on the good side. He was a little frightening.

Was it possible this man, this pirate, was content to be an executive of an agricultural company? There was a barely contained ferocity about Martin that was exciting and disturbing. I'd already known he was a competent, forceful, and decisive man, a man who made his mind up quickly and kept it made. Now he seemed more complicated.

The game was over at last, and Martin had apparently defeated the younger man, who was shaking his head ruefully. They were both pouring with sweat. I heard someone mounting the stairs heavily, then sensed a presence to my left. Someone else was standing there looking down at the racquetball court. When I glanced sideways, I saw a blond man in his forties, burly and dressed in a suit that was rather too tight. He was staring at Martin with a look that alarmed me.

When I looked back down, Martin had spotted me and was signaling that he'd be with me in ten minutes. I nodded and tried to smile. He looked puzzled, and then his eyes moved to the man next to me. Martin's grimace of recognition was irritated, no more. He gave the man a curt nod. But then his face became angry, and when I looked back at the blond man, I found out why. The man, now only three feet away, was looking at me – and not with the hate-filled glare he'd aimed at Martin but with a spiteful speculation.

I was all too aware that the hall was empty. I'd never had anyone look at me like this, and it was horrible. I was considering if the situation warranted screaming – surely the only way the exercise class would ever hear me – when I heard more footsteps thudding up the stairs. Martin, covered with sweat, said easily, 'Sam, did you want to talk to me?' He had his racket in his hand, and though his voice was relaxed, he wasn't.

'This your little squeeze, Bartell?' asked the blond man in the sort of voice you use to say insulting things.

Little squeeze?

The man hadn't decided what to do yet; I could tell by the set of his shoulders. If only I could step past him to Martin, we could simply leave. I hoped. But the burly man, who carried maybe twenty extra pounds around the middle, blocked my way. Deliberately. Now Martin's racquetball partner appeared behind Martin, and I vaguely recognized him as one of the Pan-Am Agra executives who'd been with Martin at the steak house Monday. He looked excited and interested; this was like the gunfight at the O.K. Corral.

We were all frozen for a minute.

This was absurd.

'Excuse me,' I said suddenly, clearly, and very loudly. They all jumped. The blond man halfway turned to look at me, and I just stepped right on by him, close enough to tell he'd been drinking – in the middle of the day, too! noted my puritan streak.

'Martin, we have to go to lunch, I'm starving,' I told him, and held his elbow firmly. Because I continued walking, he had to turn and the younger man had to go down the stairs ahead of me. I didn't look at Martin, and I didn't look back over my shoulder.

'I'll wait out here for you to shower,' I said at the bottom of the stairs. The blond man had not followed. I waited for Martin and his racquetball opponent to go through the doors marked MEN'S LOCKERS AND SHOWERS before I seated myself in the safe proximity of the incredible spandex girl at the reception desk.

After a moment the blond man stomped down the stairs and, giving me another long look, left.

'Do you know who that was?' I asked the receptionist. She looked up from her book – Danielle Steel, I noted – to say, 'He's not an individual member, but he used to come here on the Pan-Am Agra membership. I think his name is Sam Ulrich. They took him off the list last week, though.'

'So why didn't you tell him he couldn't come in?'

'He went too fast.' She shrugged. 'Besides, one of the guys in the men's locker room would see he wasn't on the list and tell him to leave if he went in to change.'

Security was really tight at the Athletic Club.

I stared blankly at an out-of-date magazine until Martin emerged, dressed for once in casual clothes.

When he held out his hand, I took it and rose, conscious of the receptionist's gaze. She was really making those orange-and-pink stripes ripple for Martin's benefit. But he was not in the mood.

Martin said over his shoulder to her as we left, 'I'm going to have to call the manager today. You should have informed me Sam Ulrich was in the club, and I would have escorted him out.' I caught one glimpse of her dismayed and beginning-to-be-angry face as the door swung shut.

'Are you all right?' he asked. He put his arms around me. I was kind of glad to lean against him for a moment.

'Yes. It shook me up, though,' I admitted. 'Who was that man?'

'A very recent ex-employee. Part of the deadwood I was hired to cut out of the company. He took it pretty bad.'

144

'Yes, I could tell,' I said dryly.

'I'm sorry you had to be there. If you see him again, call me instantly, okay?'

'Do you think he'd hurt me to get at you?' I asked Martin.

'Only if he's a more complete idiot than I think he is.'

Not too good an answer, really. But how could Martin tell what the man would do?

'Are you really worried about Sam?' he asked. 'Because, if so, I can cancel my trip and stay here.'

I thought for a minute. 'No, not so much worried about him, though that did shake me up. It's just been a down morning, Martin. I went to see Susu Hunter, and that was depressing. Then I went to Tonia Lee's funeral.'

'You told me when it was and I forgot. I was so involved in getting everything assembled for my trip.'

'I didn't expect you to come. It was pretty bleak, and very cold.'

'Where are we going to lunch?' he asked. 'You need something to warm you up.'

I was recalled to my hostess duties. 'Michelle's, have you been there? They have a buffet lunch with lots of vegetables.'

'In my three months here living in the motel, I think I've visited every restaurant in Lawrenceton at least ten times.'

'I didn't think about that, Martin. I'll have to cook for you soon.'

'Can you cook?'

'I have a limited repertoire,' I admitted, 'but the food is edible.'

'I like to cook once in a while,' he said.

We talked about cooking until we got to Michelle's, where we collected our plates and went through the line. I saw Martin was careful in his selections and realized he was weight- and health-conscious as well as an exercise enthusiast. We sat on the same side of the booth, and even in that prosaic setting, his nearness was disturbing.

It had been a harrowing morning, and now Martin was leaving town. Ridiculously, I felt like bursting into tears. I had to get over this. This intensity was terrifying me. I sat with my fork poised in my hand, staring straight ahead, willing myself not to cry.

'Do you want me to ignore this?' Martin murmured.

I nodded vehemently.

So he kept on quietly eating.

At last, I gathered myself together and put some cauliflower in my mouth, making myself chew and swallow.

I was going to have to keep busy while Martin was gone.

After a while I said conversationally, 'So you're leaving this afternoon?'

'About five o'clock. I'll have a meeting first thing tomorrow morning, and it may go on all day. Then I meet with another group Thursday. So I'll stay over that night and catch the first flight out Friday morning. Will you cook for me Friday night?'

'Yes,' I said, and smiled.

'And Saturday night is the Realtors' thing?'

'Yes; the annual banquet. We've booked the Carriage House, so at least the food will be good. There'll be a speaker, and cocktails. Usual stuff.'

'You handled that situation at the Athletic Club with great . . . aplomb,' he said suddenly. 'I don't think I've ever said that word out loud. But it's the only one that fits.'

'Um. I figured I could rescue myself this time.'

'Let me do it next time. My turn, okay?'

146

'Okay,' I said, and laughed.

He took me back to the Athletic Club to pick up my car, and we parted there in the parking lot. He gave me the phone number of his hotel and made me promise to call if I saw Sam Ulrich again. Then we kissed, and he was gone.

Chapter Eleven

Madeleine had a checkup at the vet's office scheduled the next morning. I got out the stout metal cage Jane had bequeathed me and opened the little door. I put one of Madeleine's toys inside. I set the cage, door open, on the kitchen table. I put on gardening gloves.

I had profited by experience.

Madeleine knew the instant the cage came out. She could find places to hide you'd swear a fat old cat could never squeeze into. I'd quietly gone upstairs first and closed all the doors while Madeleine was in plain view on the couch, and even closed off the front downstairs living room and the downstairs bathroom. But still, Madeleine had disappeared.

I groaned and started searching.

This time she'd wedged herself under the television stand.

'Come on, old girl,' I coaxed, knowing I was wasting my breath.

The battle raged for nearly twenty minutes. Madeleine and I cursed at each other, and very nearly spat at each other. But after that twenty minutes, Madeleine was in the cage, staring out with the haunted expression of a political prisoner being filmed by Amnesty International.

I dabbed some antibiotic ointment on the worst scratches and pulled on my coat. I was bracing myself for the ordeal to come.

Madeleine wailed all the way to Dr Jamerson's office. Nonstop.

Sometimes I loathed that cat.

'Oh, good, Madeleine's right on time,' said Dr Jamerson's nice receptionist with a distinct lack of enthusiasm. I returned a grim nod.

'Let's see. What does Madeleine need today?'

She knew damn good and well.

'All her shots.'

'Charlie'll get his gloves,' she said, heaving a resigned sigh. 'He'll be with you in just a minute.'

Charlie helped Dr Jamerson with the really difficult animals. He was a huge cheerful young man, working at the vet's office until he had enough saved to go to college full-time instead of part-time.

'Is she here yet?' I heard Charlie ask the receptionist apprehensively. A moment later Charlie stuck his head out into the waiting room.

'Right on time, as always, Miss Teagarden! And how is your kitty today?'

Madeleine yowled. The Labrador on the other side of the room began to whine and pressed his nose against his owner's leg. Charlie winced.

'Better bring her back,' he said with false assurance. 'Doctor's waiting.'

I struggled with the heavy carrier, knowing I'd have to heft it myself, since Madeleine had found out last time that her paw could fit through the mesh door nicely, even with her claws fully extended. Dr Jamerson had all Madeleine's shots laid out ready, plus a generous supply of cotton balls and antiseptic. His jaw was set, and he gave me a grim smile.

'Bring her on, Miss Teagarden. We got through her neutering before, we'll get through her shots now, Thank God she's a healthy cat.'

That thought certainly gave me pause. If Madeleine was like this when she felt *good* – 'Oh, dear,' I said.

I pulled my gloves back on. 'Are you ready?'

'Let's do it,' Dr Jamerson said to Charlie and me, and we all nodded simultaneously. I unlatched the cage door and pulled it open.

Fifteen minutes later I emerged from the vet's office, lugging the cage with the cat screaming triumphantly inside. She'd had her shots. And we'd pretty much had ours, too.

'He didn't bleed very much, Mother,' I said reassuringly when she called to see how Dr Jamerson was doing.

'I sold him a house. He's such a nice man,' she sighed. 'I wish you'd take that cat to Dr Caitlin. He went through Today's Homes.'

'He wouldn't see her,' I said.

'Oh.'

'What time Saturday night?' I asked. 'The banquet.'

'What did you do with your invitation?'

'It got lost or something.'

'You need a bulletin board and some thumbtacks.'

'Yes, I know. What time do we need to be there?'

'Drinks at seven, dinner at seven thirty.'

'Okay.'

'I'm going to be showing him some more houses, you know.'

'Oh – no, we didn't talk about it.'

'Nothing as grand as the Anderton place, but all in the

one to two hundred thousand range. He must be planning on doing a lot of entertaining.'

'He's the head man here. I guess so.'

'Still, a single man . . . why does he want that much room?'

'I don't know.' Because he came from a poor farm in America's heartland? I had no idea.

'Well, I hope you know what you're doing.'

'I do too,' I said softly.

'Oh, Roe, have you got it bad?' My mother was suddenly distressed.

'Yes,' I said, and closed my eyes.

'Oh, dear.'

'I'll see you Saturday night,' I said hastily. 'Bye, Mother.'

'Bye, baby.' My mother was worried.

I'd rented a movie to watch that night, and I was curled up in front of the television wrapped in a quilt and eating crackers and peanut butter when Martin called. He just wanted to see if I was okay, he told me, after the incident with Sam Ulrich the morning before. He was lonely in his hotel room, he told me.

After I hung up, I thought about his exercise equipment and his running and his racquetball, and I closed the peanut butter jar.

And before I went to bed, I thought about Sam Ulrich – and Idella and Tonia Lee – and I double-checked all my doors and windows.

I'd just pulled on my jeans and a sweater the next morning when the phone rang.

'Roe,' said the warm voice on the other end, 'how are you this morning?'

'Oh, hi, Franklin.' Mild curiosity stirred within me. 'I'm all right.'

'Not too shaken up by your dreadful experience?'

'You mean finding Idella. It was just horrible, Franklin, but I haven't dwelt on it.' I'd been dwelling on something else. I felt myself smiling, and was ashamed.

'That's good. Life goes on,' he said offhandedly. 'I called to see if by chance you would go with me to the Realtor's banquet?'

Well, well. The legendary Franklin Farrell was asking little old me for a date. He'd probably gone out with every other woman in Lawrenceton.

'Franklin, how nice of you to ask. I'm flattered. But I already have plans for that night.'

'Oh, that's too bad. Well, another time then.'

'Thanks for calling.'

If anyone had been there to see me, I would have raised my eyebrows in amazement. Franklin Farrell without a date, and the banquet so close? Something must have happened to his original plans. Did this mean someone had canceled on Franklin? That would indeed be news.

I drummed my fingers on the kitchen counter.

The next thing I knew, I was asking Patty to connect me with Eileen.

'How are you doing, honey?' Eileen asked, but without her usual boom.

'I'm just fine. You?'

'Still upset, Roe. I just can't stop seeing Idella, thrown down like a sack of garbage.'

'It had to have been quick, Eileen. Maybe she didn't know anything about it.'

The paper had quoted Lynn as saying it was believed Idella'd been strangled like Tonia Lee, though that wouldn't be a certainty until the autopsy. I did hope it had been quick, but I had a conviction that Idella had known exactly who was killing her and that she was being killed. I tried so hard not to imagine that that I bit my lip.

'I hope not,' Eileen was sighing. 'Listen, Roe, not to change the subject, but I have to get on with my work, I guess. I took yesterday off. Do you want to do any more house-hunting today?'

'I don't think so, Eileen. I've kind of lost my taste for it, for a little while at least. I liked the Julius house so much better than anything I've seen, but I have to ponder long and hard about whether I could live out of town without getting the willies every night.'

'I can understand that, believe me. Just give me a call when you make up your mind.'

'Listen, Eileen. Do you know if Idella had been dating anyone special?'

'If she was, she didn't tell me who. But she had been very "up" lately, dressing more carefully, cheerful, eyes shiny, etcetera. Idella wasn't one to talk about her personal life. I worked with her for a month without her mentioning her children!'

'She *was* closemouthed,' I said, impressed. 'I just wondered if she hadn't been dating Franklin Farrell.'

'I would be extremely surprised,' Eileen said instantly. 'You know what a reputation he has as a ladies' man. Idella was very shy.'

She'd have been a real challenge to a Franklin Farrell.

'You heard they questioned Jimmy Hunter?' Eileen told me suddenly.

'Yes, but I don't believe he's guilty.'

'It's got to be someone,' Eileen said practically. 'Though I hear his alibi for the time Idella was killed is pretty strong.'

'So there are two stranglers in Lawrenceton, attacking real estate saleswoman?'

'You've heard about copycat killers. Maybe this is one.'

'What about the thefts?'

'I'm not the police,' Eileen said irritably. 'I'm just hoping all this is over and I can go back to my job without being scared every time I have an appointment to meet someone at an empty house.'

'Sure,' I said, instantly contrite. 'I'm a friend of Susu's, or at least I used to be in high school.'

'We're not going to come out of this with everyone happy.'

'Of course not. Listen, when do you walk every evening?'

'Terry and I usually walk at five in the winter, seven in the summer. Did you want to join us?'

'Oh, how nice of you! No, I'd just slow you down. I thought I might give it a try, but I'd better go by myself at first.'

'Then be careful.'

'Okay. See you Saturday night.'

'Bye.'

I actually found myself a tiny bit regretful I wasn't going to see Franklin in action. Amina had told me a date with Franklin was like being in a warm, soothing bubble bath. You felt cherished and delicate and pamperable. And of course you wanted that to go on and on, so the date extended very easily into bed. Once or twice, or perhaps even for a month. And then Franklin stopped calling and you had to come back to the real world.

If Martin hadn't happened, I would certainly have accepted, just to sample the experience. I would have stopped short of bed, I told myself firmly.

I put out fresh food and water for Madeleine, who was still hiding somewhere in the townhouse, sulking about the great indignity done her at the vet's.

And the phone rang again.

This time it was Sally Allison.

'The police searched the Hunters' house and came up with zilch,' she said without preamble.

'Oh, thank God. Maybe he's not such a suspect anymore?'

'Could be. The afternoon Idella Yates was killed, he was in the hardware store without a break, in full view of at least three people at any given moment. And he says he did look at the Anderton house with Tonia Lee, but on a different day. That's how his fingerprints got on the night table.'

'Is it okay for you to be telling me this?'

'If you don't tell anyone else. Otherwise, Paul will have my guts for garters.'

'I understand.'

'I know you're a friend of Susu's, so I just wanted you to know.'

'Thanks, Sally. Listen, did you ever date Franklin Farrell?'

'No,' she said, and laughed. 'I didn't want to be a cliché. He tries to date you when he thinks you're especially lonely, or rebounding from a relationship, or if you're a little stupid. I understand he really wines and dines you before the Big Move, but when he called me, I was too scared I'd join the ranks to accept.'

'Just wondered.'

'Oh, did you get that newspaper article I sent you?'

'Oh, shoot. I forgot to check my mail yesterday. I'll bet it's out there. I'll go see.'

'Okay. If you don't get it, call me.'

I reached in my mailbox eagerly and came out with a handful. Yes, here was the article Sally had sent me as she'd promised. There was Martin's picture. I sighed absurdly. Martin, I read, had a background in agriculture (I assumed that was his being raised on a farm); a distinguished service record, including two purple hearts (that explained the scars I hadn't yet asked him about); and a long work history with Pan-Am Agra . . . a brief chronicle of his steady rise through the ranks followed . . . then a noncommital statement of Martin's, about his plans for the plant.

There wasn't anything much to it, really, but for some reason it was very exciting to read about my – well, whatever – in the paper. So I read it over. And over.

'Isn't that strange,' I said out loud.

Martin had mentioned casually to me that he had gotten out of the Army in 1971. This article stated that he'd begun work at Pan-Am Agra in 1973.

What had Martin been doing for those two years? I wondered.

Chapter Twelve

Little tasks consumed the rest of my day. I had to stop by the dry cleaner's and go to the grocery store with a list of ingredients for the supper I was going to cook Martin the next night. I did my laundry and a little ironing. I sent Amina and her husband a 'congratulations' card and a copy of Dr Spock's famous book on baby care.

And I went by the library to check out some books. Every time I went into my former place of employment, I felt a pang of regret. There were so many things I missed about working there: seeing all the new books first (and free), having a chance to see and learn about so many people in the town I wouldn't run across otherwise, the companionship among the librarians, just being in the presence of so many books.

What I didn't miss was the companionship of Lillian Schmidt. So of course it was Lillian who was at the checkout desk today. I politely asked after Tonia Lee's mother and got a blow-by-blow account of Mrs Purdy's collapse after the funeral and her continued depression, Mrs Purdy's relief on hearing there had been an arrest, Mrs Purdy's horror and disbelief on hearing who was being questioned, Mrs Purdy's confusion on hearing that there was no concrete proof against Jimmy Hunter.

'Oh, that's great!' I said involuntarily.

Lillian was affronted. Her oversized bosom heaved under

its striped polyester covering. 'I just think it's one of those technicalities,' she said. 'I bet they'll be sorry when some other woman gets killed in her bed.'

I forbore remarking that the bed Tonia Lee had been killed in was not exactly her own. 'If someone else does die, it won't be because Jimmy Hunter wasn't arrested,' I said firmly if confusingly, and picked up my books.

By the time I got home and unloaded my car, it was a little after four, and becoming dark and colder. This was getting close to the time of day Tonia Lee had been killed. With no other car having been seen in the driveway, the police had thought Mackie might be involved, since he ran every evening at this time. I thought the theory was sound, even though they'd had the wrong person. This evening, I'd walk myself. Just to see what could be seen.

Twenty minutes later I was shaking my head and muttering to myself. The streets were practically teeming with walkers and joggers. I had had no idea that the residential areas of Lawrenceton were so busy at an hour I normally associated with winding down and preparing supper. Every other block, it seemed, I passed another walker, or a runner, or a biker. Sometimes two. Everyone in town was out in the streets! Arms swinging energetically, Walkmans (Walkmen?) fixed on ears, expensive athletic shoes pounding the pavement . . . it was amazing.

I was heading toward the Anderton house, of course, walking at as swift a clip as I could manage. I passed Mackie, running in a sweatshirt and gym shorts, pouring sweat in the chilly air; he gave me the quick nod that was apparently all that was expected of runners. Next I saw Franklin Farrell, keeping trim for all those ladies, running at a more moderate pace, his long legs muscular and lean. No wonder he seemed so much younger than I knew he must be. True to his nature, he managed an intimate smile even through his careful breathing. Eileen and Terry marched by together, weights on their ankles and wrists, arms swinging in unison, not talking, and keeping a pace I knew would have me panting in minutes.

This was much more interesting than my exercise video. All these people, including half the real estate community, all out and about at the time the murderer must have arrived at the Anderton house. Even Mark Russell, the farm broker, strode by, in an expensive walking outfit from the Sports Kitter shop. And perfect Patty Cloud, bless my soul, in an even more expensive pale pink silky-looking running suit, her hair drawn up and back into a perky ponytail with matching pink bow. Patty even jogged correctly.

And here came Jimmy Hunter on a very fancy bike.

'Jimmy!' I said happily. He pulled to a stop and shook my hand.

'Susu told me you came by yesterday when everyone else was staying away,' he said gruffly. 'Thanks.'

'Are you okay?' I asked inadequately. He'd been through such an ordeal.

'I will be,' he said, shaking his head slightly as though a fly were circling it. 'It's going to be hard getting over this feeling that everyone was against me, that everyone believed I'd done it, right off the bat.'

'Susu okay?'

'She's tired, but she's regrouping. We have a lot to talk about. I think we'll leave the kids with their aunt and uncle for a while.'

'I hope everything—' I floundered. 'I'm really glad you're home,' I finally said.

'Thanks again, Roe,' he said, and wheeled away.

Seconds later I was in front of the Anderton house, its Select Realty sign still stuck forlornly in the yard, doomed to be frosted and snowed upon all winter and covered with the quick grass of spring and the weeds of summer, I was sure.

I didn't think the Anderton house, or the little ranch-style where we'd found Idella, would sell anytime soon.

After all, these deaths hardly seemed to be the work of a random killer, striking where he could find a woman alone.

I wondered if anyone had seen a car at the house where Idella'd been found.

A client arriving by foot would have been unusual, even unnerving, especially to Idella, who'd already been made nervous by Tonia Lee's death, who'd already heard that the police suspected someone of arriving at the Anderton house on foot . . . surely she'd have run screaming from the house instantly?

Yes, if it had been a random client who called to set up an appointment.

But not if it had been someone she knew, someone who said, maybe, 'My run (or my bike ride) takes me by there, so I'll see you at the Westley house', or something of the sort. And what more impersonal place to kill than someone else's empty house? You could just leave the body where it fell. The killer hadn't had a chance to divert suspicion, hadn't had the opportunity to move Idella's car somewhere else; since it had been dusk, not dark, when Idella had been murdered, her car couldn't have been moved without the driver being seen. Idella had had to be silenced quickly or she would have told what she knew . . . and Donnie Greenhouse thought she knew who'd killed his wife.

There he was now, as if my thinking of him had conjured him up, alternately walking and jogging, dressed in ancient dark blue sweats. He was dangerously hard to see in the gathering dark. I could just make out the features of his face.

'Roe Teagarden,' he said by way of greeting. 'What are you doing out tonight?'

'Walking, like everyone else in Lawrenceton.'

He laughed without humor. 'Decided to join the crowd, huh? I come here every evening,' he said with an abrupt change in tone. 'I come stand here while I'm out running. I think about Tonia Lee, about what she was like.'

This was weird.

A car went by, its headlights underlining the suddenly increasing darkness. I had a rather long walk home. I began to shift my feet uneasily.

'She was quite a woman, Roe. But you knew her. She was one of a kind.'

That was the absolute truth. I was able to nod emphatically.

'Everyone wanted her, and not just men, either; but she was my wife,' he told me proudly. His words had the feeling of a mantra he'd chanted over and over.

My scalp began to crawl.

'She'll never cheat with anyone else again,' Donnie said with some satisfaction.

'Um, Donnie? Do you think it's really that good for you to keep on coming over here?'

He turned to me, but I couldn't see his face well enough to discern his expression.

'Maybe not, Roe. You think I should resist the temptation?' His voice was mocking.

'Yes,' I said firmly. 'I think so. Donnie, why didn't you tell the police what you and Idella talked about that day at the restaurant?'

'So that's how they knew. Idella talked to you in the women's room.'

'She told me you were saying you saw her car come out of your office parking lot.'

'Yeah. I was out looking for Tonia Lee. So I cruised by the office. Sometimes she would take people there if she couldn't find anywhere else.'

'Was Idella driving?'

'I couldn't tell. But it was her car. It had that MY CHILD IS AN HONOR STUDENT AT LCS bumper sticker.'

'You can't believe that Idella killed Tonia Lee.'

'No, Roe, I've never believed that. But I think she gave a ride home to whomever left Tonia Lee's car at the office. And I think I know who that was.'

'You should tell the police, Donnie.'

'No, Roe, this is mine. My vengeance. I may take my time about it. But Tonia Lee would have wanted me to avenge her.'

I drew in a deep, cautious breath. The conversation could only go downhill from here. 'It's really dark, Donnie. I'd better go.'

'Yes, don't get caught alone with someone you don't know very well.'

I took a tiny step backward.

'And don't go into houses with strangers,' he added, and ran away, the measured thud of his Reeboks fading into the distance.

I headed in the opposite direction. I would have gone that way even if it hadn't been the way home.

I walked back to the townhouse more quickly than I'd set forth. It was too dark to be out by now, and my brown coat rendered me invisible to cars. I hadn't prepared very well for my walk, and I was unnerved by my encounter with Donnie. I pulled my keys out when I neared the back of my townhouse – I'd automatically walked into the parking lot instead of going to my closer but seldom-used front door. The lighting back here was good, but I glanced around carefully as I approached my patio gate.

I caught a little movement, from the corner of my eye, back by the dumpster in the far corner of the lot.

There weren't any strange cars parked under the porte cochere. All the vehicles belonged to residents. I stared into the dark corner where the Dumpster squatted. Nothing moved.

'Is anyone there?' I called, and my voice was disgracefully squeaky.

Nothing happened.

After a long moment I very reluctantly turned my back, and moving quicker than I had on my walk, I raced through my patio and turned the key in the back door, closing and shutting it behind me with even greater rapidity.

The phone was ringing.

If the caller had been Martin, I probably would have told him how scared I was. But it was my mother, wanting to know the news about the police questioning of Jimmy Hunter. I talked with her long enough to calm down, carefully not mentioning why I was so breathless. I hadn't really seen anything, and if I possibly *had* seen just a tiny movement, what I'd glimpsed was a cat prowling around the Dumpster in search of mice or scraps. There was, it was true, a murderer at large in Lawrenceton, but there was no reason on earth to believe he or she was after me. I knew nothing, had seen nothing, and was not even in real estate.

But the feeling of being observed would not leave, and I wandered restlessly around the ground floor of the town-house, making sure everything was locked and all the curtains and shades were drawn tight.

Finally, after telling myself several times in a rallying way that I was being ridiculous, I went upstairs to change. Even in the cold, I'd sweated during my walk. Normally, I would have taken a shower, but this night, I could not bring myself to step in the tub and close the shower curtain. So I pulled on my ancient heavy bathrobe, a thick saddle blanket of a robe in green-and-blue plaid, the most comforting garment I have ever known.

It didn't work its magic. I found myself scared to turn on the television for fear the noise would block out the sounds of an intruder. But nothing happened, all evening. I was caught up in some kind of siege mentality; I got a box of Cheez-Its and a diet Coke and holed up in my favorite chair, with a book I'd read many times, one of William Marshall's Yellowthread Street series. But even his endearingly bizarre plotting could not relax me.

I wondered if men had evenings like this.

The time passed, somehow. I turned on my patio and front door lights, intending to leave them burning all night. I switched off the interior lights. I went from window to window, sitting in the dark and looking out. I never saw anything else; about one o'clock, I heard a car start up somewhere close and drive away. Though that could have signaled any number of things, perhaps none of them concerning me, I was able to sleep in fits and starts after that.

Chapter Thirteen

It was raining Friday evening when Martin came to supper. He had barely shed his raincoat when he gathered me up in his arms.

'Martin,' I whispered, finally.

'Humm?'

'The water for the spaghetti is boiling over.'

'What?'

'Let me go put in the spaghetti so we can eat. After all, you need to build up your strength.'

Which earned me a narrow-eyed look.

I can never manage to get all the elements of a meal ready simultaneously, but we did eventually eat our salad and garlic bread and spaghetti with meat sauce. Martin seemed to enjoy them, to my relief. While we ate, he told me about his trip, which seemed to have consisted mainly of small enclosed spaces alternating with large enclosed spaces: airplane, airport, meeting room, dining room, hotel room, airport, airplane.

When he asked me what I'd been doing, I almost told him I'd sat up last night afraid of the bogey man. But I didn't want Martin to think of me as a shaking, trembly kind of woman. Instead, I told him about my walk, about the people I'd seen.

'And they all had a chance to kill Tonia Lee,' I said. 'Any one of them could have walked up to the house in the dusk.

Tonia Lee wouldn't have been too surprised to see any one of them, at least initially.'

'But it had to have been a man,' suggested Martin. 'Don't you think?'

'We don't know if she'd actually had sex,' I pointed out. 'She was positioned to look like it, but we don't have the postmortem report. Or she could have had sex, and then been killed by someone other than her sex partner.' Martin seemed to take this conversation quite matter-of-factly.

'That would assume a lot of traffic in and out of the Anderton house.'

'Doesn't seem too likely, does it? But it could be. After all, the presence of a woman wouldn't scare Tonia Lee at all. And Donnie Greenhouse said several very strange things last night.' I told Martin about Donnie's remark that not only men had wanted Tonia Lee, and about his sighting of Idella's car. But I didn't say anything about Eileen and Terry; just because they were the only lesbians I knew about in Lawrenceton didn't mean they were the only ones in town.

Aubrey would have been nauseated by this time.

'So what's your assumption?' Martin asked.

'I think . . . I think Tonia Lee learned who was stealing those things from the houses for sale. I think she was having an affair with whoever it was, or he – or she – seduced her when she asked him to come to the Anderton house to talk about the thefts. Maybe he asked her to meet him under the guise of having a romp in the hay there, when he meant to finish her all along. So they romp or they don't, but either way he fixes it to look as if they had. I'm sure he planned it beforehand. He arrives by foot or bicycle, he kills Tonia Lee, he positions her sexually to make us think it's just one of her paramours who got exasperated, he moves her car, he goes home, he somehow gets the key back to our key board. He thinks that that way no one will look for Tonia Lee for days, days during which all alibis will be blurred or forgotten or unverifiable. Maybe he returns the key in the few minutes Patty and Debbie are both out of the front room at the office.'

Martin had been listening quietly, thinking along with me. Now he held up his hand.

'No,' he said. 'I think Idella must have put back the key.'

'Oh, my God, yes. Idella,' I said slowly. 'That's why he killed her. She knew who had had the key. She got it from whoever was at Greenhouse Realty.'

That made so much sense. Idella, crying at the staff meeting right after Tonia's body was discovered. Idella, red-eyed and upset during the days after the killing.

'It must have been someone she was incredibly loyal to,' I murmured. 'Why wouldn't she tell? It would have saved her life.'

'She couldn't believe it, she wouldn't believe this person did it,' Martin said practically. 'She was in love.'

We stared at each other for a minute.

'Yes,' I said quietly. 'That must have been it. She must have been in love.'

I thought of Idella after Martin fell asleep that night. Deluded in the most cruel way, Idella had died at the hands of someone she loved, someone of whom she could believe no evil, no matter how compelling the evidence. In a way, I thought drowsily, Idella had been like me . . . she'd been alone for a while, coping with her life on her own. Maybe that had made her all too ready to trust, to depend.

It had cost her everything. I prayed for her, for her children, and finally for Martin and me.

I must have coasted off into sleep, because the next thing I was aware of was waking. I woke up just a little, though; just enough to realize I'd been asleep, just enough to realize something unusual had roused me.

I could hear someone moving very quietly downstairs. Martin must be getting a drink and doesn't want to disturb me – so sweet, I thought drowsily, and turned over on my stomach, pillowing my face on my bent arms. My elbow touched something solid.

Martin.

My eyes opened wide in the darkness.

I froze, listening.

The slight sound from downstairs was repeated. I automatically reached out to the night table for my glasses and put them on.

I could see the darkness much more clearly.

I slid out of bed as silently as I could, my slithery black nightgown actually of some practical use, and crept to the head of the stairs. Maybe it was Madeleine? Had I fed her before we came up to bed?

But Madeleine was in her usual night place, curled on the little cushioned chair by the window, and she was sitting up, her head turned to the doorway. I could see the profile of her ears against the faint light of the streetlamp a block north on Parson Road, coming in through the blinds.

I glided back to the bed, very careful not to stumble over scattered clothes and shoes.

'Martin,' I whispered. I leaned over my side of the bed and touched his arm. 'Martin, there's trouble. Wake up.'

'What?' he answered instantly, quietly.

'Someone downstairs.'

'Get behind the chair,' he said almost inaudibly, but very urgently.

I heard him get out of bed, heard him – just barely heard him – feeling in his overnight bag.

I was ready to disobey and take my part in grabbing the intruder – after all, this was my house – when I saw in that little bit of glow from the streetlight that Martin was holding a gun.

Well, it did seem time to get behind something. Actually, the chair felt barely adequate all of a sudden. I left Madeleine right where she was. Not only would she very probably have yowled if I'd grabbed her, but I trusted her survival instincts far more than mine.

I strained as hard as I could to hear but detected only some tiny suggestions of movement – maybe Martin going to the head of the stairs. Despite the dreadful hammering of my heart, I said a few earnest prayers. My legs were shaking from fear and the cramped crouching position I'd assumed.

I willed myself to be still. It worked only a little, but I could hear some sounds coming up the stairs. This intruder was no skilled stalker.

I found I was more frightened of what Martin might do than I was of the intruder. Only slightly, though.

I heard the someone enter the room. I covered my face with my hands.

And the lights came on.

'Stop right there,' Martin said in a deadly voice. 'I have a gun pointed at your back.'

I peeked around the chair. Sam Ulrich was standing inside the room with his back to Martin, who was pressed against the wall by the light switch. Ulrich had a length of rope in one hand, some wide masking tape in the other. His face was livid with shock and excitement. Mounting my stairs must have been pretty heart-pounding for him, too.

'Turn around,' Martin said. Ulrich did. 'Sit on the end of the bed,' Martin said next. The burly ex-Pan-Am Agra executive inched back and sat down. Slowly I got up from my place behind the chair, finding out that during those few moments I'd spent there, my muscles had become strained and sore from the tension. My legs were shaking, and I decided sitting in the chair would be a good idea. My robe was draped over the back of it, and I pulled it on. Madeleine had vanished, doubtless irritated at having her night's sleep so rudely interrupted.

'Are you all right, Roe?' Martin asked.

'Okay,' I said shakily.

We stared at our captive. I had a thought. 'Martin, where did you park when you came tonight? Are you in your car?'

'No,' he said slowly. 'No, I parked out back in one of the parking slots, but I'm in a company car. I don't like to leave my car parked at the airport.'

'So he didn't know you were here,' I observed.

Martin absorbed that quickly. From looking perplexed and angry, his expression went to murderous.

'What were you going to do with the rope and the tape, Sam?' he asked very quietly.

I felt all the blood drain from my face. I hadn't followed through on my own idea until Martin asked that critical question.

'You son of a bitch, I was going to hurt you like you hurt me,' Sam Ulrich said savagely.

'I didn't rape your wife.'

'I wasn't going to rape her,' he said, as if I weren't there.

171

'I was going to scare her and leave her tied up so you'd know what it was like to see your family helpless.'

'Your logic escapes me,' Martin said, and his voice was like a brand-new razor blade.

I knew this was a quarrel between the two men, but after all, it was I who would have been tied up.

'Didn't you feel it might be a little cowardly,' I said clearly, 'to creep up in the dark and tie up a woman who wasn't even your real enemy?'

It seemed Sam Ulrich had never put it to himself quite that way. He turned even redder in a slow, ugly way.

'I'd like to kill you,' Martin said very quietly. I didn't doubt his sincerity, and I could tell from the hunch of his shoulders that Ulrich didn't, either. Martin, even in pajama bottoms, had more authority than Sam Ulrich would have had in a suit. 'But since it's Roe's house you broke into, and her you were going to harm, maybe she should decide what should happen to you.'

I knew that Martin would kill this man if I asked him to.

I thought of calling the police. I thought of cops I knew from having dated Arthur, perhaps even Arthur himself, up here in my bedroom looking at me in my black nightie. I thought of their eyes as they found out Martin and I had been asleep together when I heard someone downstairs. I thought of the report taken from the police blotter that appeared daily in the Lawrenceton *Sentinel*. Then I thought of letting this dreadful coward go scot-free. But my flesh crawled when I pictured myself alone here with this frustrated man and his rope and his tape.

And I'll tell you what I just plain liked about Martin. He let me think. He didn't say one word, or look impatient, or even make a face.

'Do you have a wife?' I asked Sam Ulrich.

'Yes,' he mumbled.

'Children?'

'Two.'

'What are their names?'

He looked more and more humiliated. 'Jannie and Lisa,' he said reluctantly.

'Jannie and Lisa wouldn't like to see their father's name in the paper for attacking an unarmed woman in her home.'

I thought that between anger and humiliation he might cry.

I got a pen and a notepad from my bedside drawer.

'Write,' I said.

He took the pen and paper.

'Date it.'

He wrote the date.

'I am dictating this now. Start writing,' I told him. 'I, Sam Ulrich, broke into the townhouse of Aurora Teagarden tonight . . .' His hand finally moved. When it stopped, I continued. 'I had with me some rope and masking tape.' Done. 'She was asleep in bed with all the lights out, and I did not know anyone was in the townhouse with her.' His fingers moved even slower. 'I was only prevented by her house guest from doing her harm. If I do not abide by the conditions she sets forth, she will send this letter to the police, with a copy to my wife.' And as he finished writing, I told him to sign it.

He waited to hear my conditions.

'What I want to see is your house up for sale tomorrow, and for God's sake don't list it with Select Realty. And I want you out of here, moved, family and all, within the week. I never want you to come back here, and I never want to see you again. You may not get a job like you're used to, but anything, I think, would be better than being in jail for what you wanted to do to me.'

Martin's face was blank.

Ulrich was so upset his features were distorted. I wondered if between rage, and relief, and shock, he would have a heart attack on the way home, and I found myself not much caring if he did.

'Martin, could you please walk Mr Ulrich to his car?'

'Sure, honey,' Martin agreed, with a dangerous kind of smoothness. 'Come on, Ulrich. You're lucky I asked the lady. I would have put you in the hospital if it had been up to me.'

Or the morgue, I thought.

Sam Ulrich rose slowly. He took a step forward and then stopped. He was afraid to go closer to Martin. He was not such a fool as he looked. Martin moved back, and Ulrich preceded him down the stairs.

I heard the back door open and close, and wondered if I'd left it unlocked when we'd gone upstairs for the night. I didn't think so. Not a very good lock. I'd get a better one.

Being left alone for a few minutes was a great relief, and I burst into tears and tried very hard not to picture myself at the mercy of the man now being marched to his car.

I was rinsing my face at the sink, the cold water making me shudder, when Martin returned. I saw his reflection in the mirror beside mine.

'You've been crying,' he said very gently, putting his gun on my vanity table, where it lay looking as out of place as a rattlesnake. I turned and put my arms around him. His bare chest was cold from the outside air, and I rubbed my cheek against him.

'He's driving home,' he said, answering a question I was scared to ask.

'Martin,' I said, 'if you hadn't been here . . .'

'You would have called 911, because I wouldn't have been between you and the phone,' he said practically. 'They would have been here in two minutes, maximum, and you would have been fine.'

'So this doesn't count as a rescue?' I asked shakily.

'We're even on this one. You kept me from doing something stupid to him. I would hate to have to spend the night down at the police station because of Sam Ulrich. You saved his family, too.'

'Martin. Let's just get in bed and pile all the blankets on, and you can hold me.'

I was trembling from head to toe. I realized, as I lay with my eyes wide open in the dark, that I had had to wait to find that Sam Ulrich had left in his own car – alive – before I could let myself have the luxury of relaxing, believing the incident was over. Martin was awake, too, listening. I didn't think Ulrich was stupid enough to come back; he should be in his own bed counting his blessings.

I began to count my own.

At least Martin didn't try to get to the plant early on Saturday, but he felt he should go in, especially since he'd been out of town. 'I think my weekend hours will decrease now things are beginning to shape up at this plant,' he told me over our morning coffee, 'especially now that I have a reason to stay away.'

I tried to smile back, but my attempt must have been a miserable failure.

'Roe,' he said seriously, 'it's me that got you into the

trouble last night, and for that I am so sorry. He wouldn't have come here if it wasn't for me. I hope you don't hate me for that.'

'No,' I said, surprised. 'No, never think it. I'm just tired, and it was very upsetting. And you know – you do have to tell me why you brought a gun when you came to spend the night with me.'

'I've had a hard life,' Martin said after a moment. 'I have a job that requires me to do difficult things to other people, people like Ulrich.'

I closed my eyes briefly. This was all probably true, as far as it went. 'All right,' I said.

'Do you think you'll feel like going to that banquet tonight?'

I'd forgotten all about it. Of course, I wasn't wild about going, but on the other hand, when I pictured my mother asking me why we hadn't come, I just couldn't come up with a believable excuse.

'I guess so,' I said unenthusiastically. 'I'd rather drag myself there than think about last night.'

'Don't forget to wear your hair up,' Martin reminded me later as he gathered all his things to stow in his company car. 'What time should I come by?'

'I think cocktails start at six thirty.'

'Six thirty it is. Dressy?'

'Yes. Everyone can bring two other couples as guests, so there's usually a decent crowd, and there's a speaker.'

I was leaning on the door frame, and Martin was halfway to his car when he dropped the things he was carrying and came back. He held my hand.

'You aren't off me because of last night?' He looked at me steadily as he asked.

I shook my head slowly, trying to analyze what I did feel, why things seemed so grim. 'I just realized I'd taken on more than I'd anticipated,' I said, giving him the condensed version.

He looked at me quizzically. I was so tired that my judgment was impaired, and I went on. 'You're a dangerous man, Martin,' I said.

'Not to you,' he told me. 'Not to you.'

Especially to me, I thought, as I watched him drive away.

I had completely forgotten to make an appointment to get my hair put up. Of course, all the hairdressers who were open on Saturday were fully booked. But with some wheedling and bribing, I got my mother's regular woman to stay open late to work with my mane. I would be done barely in time for the dinner.

That suited me just fine. I climbed wearily up my stairs and went back to bed. It was becoming a habit.

When I woke again at two o'clock, the gray day didn't look any more inviting, but I felt much better. I decided to cram the night before into a mental closet for the time being, to take some pleasure in going to a social function in Lawrenceton with Martin for the first time. I was human enough to relish the anticipation of eyebrows lifted, of envious women. I was convinced any woman with hormones would want Martin.

I even turned on my exercise tape and got at least halfway through it before getting fed up with the dictatorial instructress. Madeleine watched me, as usual, her eyes round and disbelieving. She followed me upstairs for my shower, watched me put on my makeup and dry my hair. I changed my sheets, too, and ran a carpet sweeper over the bedroom hurriedly.

I would be running so short on time I decided to put on everything but the actual dress before I left for my hair appointment. So I looked through my closets. I'd wear the dress I'd worn the year before. Martin hadn't seen it, even if everyone else had, and I'd only worn it that once. It was green, and after simple long sleeves and a scoop neck, the bodice descended to a point in front, and the short skirt flounced out in gathers all around. I'd have to wear black heels . . . I needed some of those shiny lamé-looking shoes that were so popular now, but I didn't have the energy or time to go shopping. Black would have to do. I had a little black evening purse, too. So I put on the right bra and slip and hose, and a dress that buttoned down the front over them.

I hurried out to my car and started across town to my mother's hairdresser. I'd looked up an address before leaving home, and I took a little detour. There was the Ulrich house, a three-bedroom ranch style in one of Lawrenceton's prettier middle-class neighborhoods.

And there was a FOR SALE sign in the yard.

Chapter Fourteen

'How do you want it done?' Benita asked briskly. It was clearly the end of a long day for her. Her own red hair was wild and dark at the roots, and the beige-and-blue uniform all the operators at Clip Casa wore was rumpled and – well, hairy.

'Could you do it like this?' I'd spent my waiting time leafing through professional magazines.

'Yes,' Benita said briefly after a thorough look at the enigmatically smiling model, and set to work.

It was one of those hairdos with the braid miraculously inside-out. French braiding, I thought it was called. I'd never understood how that was done, and now it was about to be accomplished on my very own head. In the picture the model's hair wasn't pulled back tightly but puffed around her face. The length of hair at the base of the neck was also braided, and the model had a ribbon around the end. I had no fancy bows, but Benita had some for sale, including a gold lamé one I thought would be pretty. I didn't know if Martin would like the hairstyle, but it struck me as very fashionable. Plus, it didn't seem possible that my hair could come loose, as all too often happened when I put it up myself.

'Roe,' drawled a voice close by, and I recognized the apparition under the dryer as my beautiful friend Lizanne Buckley.

'I haven't seen you in a coon's age!' I said happily. 'How are you doing?'

'Just fine,' said Lizanne in her slow sweet way. 'And you?'

'Pretty good. What have you been doing?'

'Oh, I'm still down at the power company,' she said contentedly. 'And I'm still dating our local representative.'

Lawyer J. T. (Bubba) Sewell, whom I'd met in a professional capacity, would be home from the Capitol for the weekend, and he and Lizanne were also going to the Realtors' banquet, she told me. In fact, Bubba was the speaker.

'Are you two engaged?' I asked. 'That's what someone told me, but I wanted to hear it straight from the horse's mouth.'

Lizanne smiled. She had a habit of that. She was stunningly beautiful, and no slave to the bone-thin convention of female figures. She was just right. 'Oh, I expect we are,' she said.

'Someone's finally going to walk you down the aisle,' I marveled. Men had tried for years to marry Lizanne and she would have none of it, the world being the unfair place it is.

'Oh, I don't think we'll get married in a church,' Lizanne demurred. 'I haven't been in one since Mamma and Daddy died, and I don't expect to go. I believe Bubba sees that as my only drawback, a politician's wife not going to church.'

There was no possible response, and Lizanne didn't expect any. I felt like someone who was walking over a familiar sunny beach, only to discover that it had changed into quicksand.

'I hear you've been dating that new man at Pan-Am Agra,' Lizanne said after a few minutes. Lizanne heard everything.

'Yes.'

'He coming with you tonight?'

I nodded until a sharp exclamation from Benita reminded me to hold still.

'I'll be glad to meet him; I've heard a lot about him.'

I didn't know if I wanted to hear or not. 'Oh?' I said finally.

'He's got everyone out there shivering in their shoes. There's evidently been a lot of slack and some thieving, and he was sent in to be the man to get everything straight. He's firing and moving around people and looking into everything.'

Lizanne reached back and turned off her dryer, lifting the hood to reveal a head covered with large rollers. She patted them to make sure her hair was dry, took one down experimentally, nodded. 'Janie, I'm done,' she called to the beige-and-blue-uniformed beautician drinking a cup of coffee in the back of the shop. The phone rang, and Janie answered it. It was for Benita, one of her children with a household emergency, and with an exclamation of impatience, she ran to take the call. I noticed the whole time she talked, she worked on her hair with a comb she picked up from the counter; if Benita was standing, she was working on hair.

'I have a friend at the police station,' Lizanne said casually, standing by my chair and looking into my mirror. 'Jack Burns – your good buddy, Roe – has decided that since no one has been killing Realtors until now, the murderer must be someone new to town. Some of the detectives don't agree, but since they questioned Jimmy Hunter and let him go, all kinds of people have been pressuring the chief of police to find someone else. Jimmy Hunter's parents have got lots of friends in this town, and the arrest of someone else would take the suspicion off Jimmy for good. So I hear the police are going to make an arrest soon in the murders of those two women. They're probably going to be taking someone in for questioning tomorrow.'

My eyes met Lizanne's in the mirror. She was giving me a message. But I had to decipher it.

'My goodness, Lizanne Buckley!' exclaimed Benita, coming back at that inopportune moment. 'Who told you that?'

'Little bird,' Lizanne said laconically, and wandered off to her beautician's station, where she began to remove her own rollers, tossing them in one of the wheeled bins. Janie drained her cup and unhurriedly began helping Lizanne, whose easygoing attitude seemed to rub off on people. I remembered Bubba Sewell's slow good-ole-boy manner and his sharp brain and decided (in a remote corner of my own brain) that he and Lizanne would make a most interesting couple.

But mostly I was trying to figure out what Lizanne had meant.

We'd been talking about Martin. Then she'd talked about the arrest. Surely she didn't mean the police suspected Martin?

She had been letting me know Martin was going to be arrested. At the least, taken in and questioned.

I stared at the mirror as two spots of color rose to stain my cheeks. I was gripping the padded arms of the swivel chair with undue force.

'Honey, are you cold?' Benita asked. 'I can sure turn up the heat.'

'Oh. No, I'm fine, thanks.'

Ridiculous. This was ridiculous.

The police had been wrong once. They were wrong again. Of course they were wrong again, I told myself fiercely. The thefts. They'd begun long before Martin had moved here.

But the murders, of course, had begun after.

I remembered my mother wondering what on earth Martin was doing looking at such a large house. Logically, a bachelor would be looking at a smaller place, not a virtual mansion like the Anderton house. The police might think he'd made an appointment to see the Anderton house because he wanted his handiwork found. Martin had been in town some weeks before I met him, long enough to meet Tonia Lee and Idella. Tonia Lee, who would go to bed with almost anyone, would undoubtedly have licked her chops when she met Martin. Idella, wispy, palely pretty, and lonely, would have been thrilled to meet someone who could pay such close and flattering attention to her.

Of course, that was what the *police* might think.

I shut my eyes.

'Are you okay, sweetie?' Benita was asking with concern.

'I'm fine,' I lied automatically. 'Are we about finished?'

'Just about. Do you like it?'

'It's different,' I said, startled enough to peek out from under my personal black cloud. 'Gosh, I don't look like me.'

'I know,' said Benita proudly. 'You look very sleek and sophisticated. Just beautiful.'

'Gee,' I said slowly. 'I do.'

'All you need to do is go home and put on your dress and some lipstick, and you'll be ready to step out.'

I did need lipstick. And I needed some spine, too, I decided grimly. I wasn't going to let these black thoughts overwhelm me. I *knew* Martin, on some level, knew him thoroughly.

I thought.

I paid Benita handsomely, and went home to slide into my green flouncy dress and put on some lipstick. I'm going to go and have a good time, I told myself. I'm going with a handsome, sexy man who considers me absolutely necessary. He might have wanted to kill nasty Sam Ulrich last night, but he wouldn't have killed Tonia Lee and Idella. Absolutely not.

At least my inner turmoil wasn't showing on the outside. When I looked in my bathroom mirror to put on my bronzy lipstick, I looked just as good as I had in the beauty shop.

I almost wished I'd polished my nails, but that would have been absolutely out of character; and with my hair put up, I hardly knew myself, as it was.

Instead of bustling around thinking of something to do, I sat on the ottoman in front of my favorite chair, my current book lying neglected on the table beside it. I decided to pop the dress on at the last second. It hung on the bathroom door, looking festive and fancy, mocking me. I stared into space and thought about Martin gone, Martin in jail, Martin on trial.

He was as necessary to me as he said I was to him.

When the doorbell rang, it actually surprised me. I pulled off my robe, pulled the dress over my head, and zipped it up in record time. I slid my feet into my high-heeled pumps and pulled myself together to answer the door, wondering vaguely why everything looked so funny.

Martin took in a deep breath when I opened the door. He looked down at me with some unreadable emotion.

'Do I look all right?' I asked, suddenly anxious.

'Oh, yes,' he said. 'Oh, yes.'

'Do you like the hair?' I asked nervously when he still stared.

'Yes . . . very much.' He finally stepped in so I could close the door against the cold. He was wearing a black overcoat, and his white hair was strikingly attractive.

Once again I had the unsettling feeling that he was grown up and I wasn't.

'Where are your glasses?'

'Oh,' I exclaimed, 'that's why everything looked so funny.' In some relief, I found them on the little table beside my chair and popped them on. 'I tried contact lenses,' I told him defensively, 'but I'm one of those people who can't wear them. They just drove me crazy.'

'I'm glad you wear glasses.'

'Why?'

'So no one else can see you with them off,' he said, and bent to give me a kiss on the cheek. His finger traced the line of my neck. I shivered. My fears abated now that I was with him. When I was close to him, I felt that Martin would not *let* himself be arrested.

'Come look in the bathroom mirror,' he suggested.

'What?'

'Just for a minute; come with me.'

'Is my hair coming down?' My hands flew up.

'No, no,' Martin said, and smiled.

So into the bathroom we went, and I looked at myself in the mirror, Martin's face rising neatly above mine in the reflection. He pulled off his gloves, and his hand went into a pocket.

Suddenly I realized I should be absolutely terrified.

But if he wanted to kill me, he would. I took a deep breath, looking steadily at his eyes in the mirror, and from his pocket he pulled a little gray velvet box and set it on the counter. Gently and expertly he removed my earrings, plain gold balls, and opening the velvet box, he extracted gorgeous amethyst-and-diamond earrings and with no fumbling at all fixed them in my ears.

'Oh, Martin,' I said, stunned. I felt as if I'd put on my brakes at the edge of a precipice.

'Sweetheart, do you like them?' he said finally.

'Oh, yes,' I said, trying hard not to cry. 'Yes, Martin. They're beautiful.' My hands were shaking, and I clenched my fists so he wouldn't notice.

'Didn't you tell me November was your birthday?'

'Yes, it is.'

'And here it is November. I didn't know which day, but I wanted to get you a present. I know topaz is your birthstone, but none I saw seemed warm enough to me. These look like you. If you didn't know it, you look beautiful tonight.'

The stones glittered. The amethysts were rectangular and edged with small diamonds.

'I'm overwhelmed. Martin, I don't know what to say.' I'd never spoken truer words.

'Tell me you love me.'

I looked into the mirror.

'I love you.'

'That's all I wanted to hear.'

'Martin.'

His hand touched my cheek.

'Do you—?'

'Yes,' he said into my ear, kissing my neck. 'Oh, yes. I love you.'

After a while he said, 'Do we have to go?'

'Unless we want my mother coming here to find out what happened to me, yes.'

Actually, I needed a space to think, to calm down. If we stayed here, I certainly wouldn't get it.

Talk about warring emotions. Someone loved me. I loved him back. He might be questioned tomorrow for murder. He'd given me the most romantic gift, the kind women wait a lifetime for. And I'd thought for a moment that he was going to strangle me.

Martin fetched my coat from the closet while I re-examined my earrings in the mirror. 'Can you stop looking long enough to put on your coat?' he asked, laughing.

'I guess so,' I said reluctantly. The moment of terror was oozing out and filling up with delight. 'Martin, what's that clipped to your coat pocket?'

'Oh, a beeper. We've been having trouble with a particular man on the night shift. His supervisor is watching him tonight, and if he catches him stealing, he's going to beep me so I can go have it out with the guy.'

In my now almost complete wave of euphoria, I did a Scarlett O'Hara and decided to think about the bad stuff later. Maybe I couldn't put it off until tomorrow, but I could savor this minute, surely.

Martin and I were a little late, among the last to arrive. We picked glasses of white wine off the tray a waiter carried by. I spotted Lizanne and Bubba Sewell immediately. Lizanne did not hint in her greeting to me that she had given me a warning that afternoon. Maybe her liquid dark eyes rested on me a little sadly, but that was all. Bubba started one of those conversations with Martin designed to link them in the male network: he connected what he was working on as a representative with what Martin was trying to achieve at Pan-Am Agra, he told Martin that he could call him any time he wanted to 'talk things over', he illustrated his intelligence and grasp of Pan-Am Agra's interests, and he implied that Martin was the best thing that had happened to the company since sliced bread.

Martin responded cautiously but with interest.

Lizanne told me how pretty my hair looked, and admired my earrings.

'Martin gave them to me,' I said proudly.

She looked worried for a minute, then properly complimented me and drew Bubba's attention to them.

'Did you show them your ring?' he responded after a token remark.

Lizanne, with her lovely slow smile, held out her hand on which glittered a notable diamond. 'My engagement ring,' she said calmly.

'Oh,' I said. 'Oh, Lizanne, it's beautiful.' I sighed, suddenly realized I was doing so, and tried to make it silent. 'When's the wedding?'

'In the spring,' Lizanne said offhandedly. 'We've got to sit down with a calendar and pick a date. It depends on the legislature, and of course I have to give notice at my job.'

'You're quitting work?' I didn't mean to sound startled, but I was. What on earth would Lizanne do all day?

'Oh, yes. We're going to be living in my house for a while, until Bubba's career plans are finalized, but there's a lot I need to do to it . . . and I'm bored with my job anyway.'

I hadn't known boredom was a concept Lizanne

understood. Also, Lizanne heard every bit of news in her job, since the power company was a place everyone had to go sooner or later, and she had the most amazing capacity to attract confidences. I would have supposed Bubba would want Lizanne right where she was.

'Congratulations, Lizanne,' I said quietly as Bubba drew Martin off to meet another Lawrenceton mover and shaker.

She bent down to kiss me on the cheek. 'Thanks, honey,' she murmured. Then she whispered, 'They're going to take your friend in tomorrow for questioning. For sure. I'm not going to tell you how I know.'

That was why she was so popular. She never told how she knew. And she certainly hadn't told her fiancé; otherwise, he wouldn't be sucking up to Martin. He'd be avoiding him as though Martin were a leper.

'Thanks, Lizanne,' I said in almost as low a voice. Suddenly curious, I asked, 'Why are you telling me?'

'You helped me the day my parents were killed.'

I nodded, and pressed her hand. I had never been sure Lizanne had been aware of my presence or my identity on that horrible day. She and I gave each other a look and drifted apart, and I strolled over to my mother, my wineglass clutched in a death grip.

'Where'd you get the earrings?' she asked instantly. 'They're gorgeous.'

'Martin gave them to me tonight,' I said numbly, turning my head from side to side so she could get the full effect, all the time wondering what I could do to prevent tomorrow from happening.

'He did?' Mother raised her perfect brows. 'But you've only known each other such a short time!'

I shrugged.

'Oh, you have got it bad,' she said darkly. 'But at least he does, too. They're very nice, dear.'

'What are you admiring, Mrs Queensland?' Patty Cloud, in her favorite pink, this time a rose shade, appeared at my mother's shoulder, trailing a delicate cloud of expensive perfume and a staggeringly handsome date, some man from Atlanta she'd met at a Sierra Club meeting, she managed to let me know. I talked to them for a few minutes of stultifying conversation about white-water canoeing before Martin rescued me.

'How'd you get along with Bubba Sewell?' I murmured as we went to our places around the table.

'He's on the rise,' Martin said thoughtfully. 'I won't be surprised if he makes U.S. Senate some day.'

'Really?' I tried not to sound skeptical.

'He's doing everything right. A lawyer, but not a criminal lawyer. Comes from a local family with a clean record, worked himself through law school, practiced for a while before running, going to marry a beautiful wife who can't possibly offend anyone. She's planning to quit work and stay at home, producing the right picture, and I bet they have a baby before they've been married two years. It'll look good on the campaign poster, a family picture.'

I tried to think about this, to care about Bubba's career, all the while turning nonsensical schemes over in my mind. I should tell Martin. Then he could brace himself. Or run. (I staved that thought off.) I should *not* tell Martin, so he would show unfeigned surprise when the police came to Pan-Am Agra. I pictured Martin being taken from his office, his humiliation; at least the people who worked for him would see it as humiliation. I checked the rein on my imagination; surely the police could not arrest him without warning, on the little or no evidence they had. But still . . .

Of all the people I knew, the one best qualified to fend for himself was Martin. Why was I worrying?

I yanked myself out of this anxious silent yammering to introduce Martin to Franklin Farrell and his date, who were seated across from us. Franklin must have been calling his reserve list, the day he'd called me; maybe this woman had been next, in alphabetical order. She was in her late forties, remarkably well groomed and dressed. Physically she was a good match for the immaculate Franklin. She glittered in a hard way, and her practiced conversation aroused my instant distrust. Her name I didn't catch, but she was full of glib comments that gave no clue to her character. She was playing up to Franklin in a rather desperate way, and I could tell they hadn't been out together before. He was being courteously cool.

The meal was served, and I talked to Mackie on my left, and Martin on my right, and Franklin and Miss Glitter across the way, though what I said I couldn't have told you afterward.

Even through the worry, I could tell Martin and I were attracting a certain amount of attention. The tables had been arranged in a large U. Martin and I were seated on the outside of one arm of the U, and as Franklin bent to retrieve his lady friend's napkin, I realized someone across from us at the far side of the U's other arm was staring. With some amazement, I recognized my former flame Arthur Smith sitting with his wife, homicide detective Lynn Liggett Smith. Who on earth had invited them? Arthur was looking at me with all too apparent concern, his fair brows drawn together and his fingers drumming on the table. Lynn was eating and listening to Eileen Norris, who had come in with Terry, announcing to the room at large that the single ladies had just decided to come together.

I raised my eyebrows very slightly, and Arthur looked down, flushing red.

I knew then that Lizanne was right. Martin was under suspicion. Perhaps I hadn't been quite sure Lizanne had gotten the true word before, but I knew it now.

'Are you all right?' Martin asked me.

'I'm all right. I need to—' I started to say 'talk to you later,' but what an irritating thing that is to do to someone. 'I'm fine,' I said clearly. 'Do you like this salad?'

'Too much vinegar in the dressing,' he said critically, but his sharp look told me he knew something was in the wind.

Somehow I did the right things through the meal, but when Bubba got up to make his address about new legislation for the real estate industry, I was able to tune out completely. In fact, it was hard to keep my eyes aimed in the right direction. I gnawed at my problem, poked at my fear, which was like a monster with many faces; I was afraid of Martin's getting arrested, afraid of losing him, afraid of what it would do to his job and self-esteem to be questioned at the police station; and maybe afraid he was guilty.

My eyes traveled across the faces around the Carriage House's elaborate wine-and-cream banquet room. All these faces, almost all familiar. One of these people was most probably the person the police really wanted, if I could just make them see it.

The murderer was a Realtor, or connected with realty in some way – someone who'd known how to get the key replaced.

The murderer had been able to arrive at the Anderton

192

house without a car and had been part of the scenery while doing so – someone who ordinarily walked or jogged or biked in the evening.

The murderer had to be someone Idella Yates trusted, someone she'd been willing to risk a lot for, since it seemed pretty certain Idella had replaced the key.

I looked at Mackie's dark neck as he turned his face politely to the speaker. His date beyond him was picking at her nails, though she, too, was keeping a courteous face turned in the right direction. Across the room, Eileen was dabbing her lips with her napkin. Beside her, Terry, in a dark blue dress with big fake diamond buttons, was listening to Bubba with a skeptical lift to one corner of her mouth. Mark Russell and his wife were sitting with the practiced posture of those who listen to many speakers; his partner, Jamie Dietrich, a lanky man with a huge Adam's apple, stifled a yawn. Patty was all attention, though her date was doing something surreptitious under the tablecloth that brought a tiny secret smile to her face. Even young Debbie Lincoln, more beads woven into her hair than I would have thought possible, was turned to Bubba and trying to pay attention, though her date was openly, elaborately bored. Conspicuously alone, Donnie Greenhouse had deliberately left an empty chair beside him to remind people that he was a brand-new widower. Somehow I'd known he wouldn't miss an opportunity to star in a public drama, even if he had to point it out himself.

Close to Lizanne, my mother inclined her head regally to one side, her resemblance to Lauren Bacall especially pronounced. John was resting his arm on the back of her chair. John looked ready to go home. Across the table from Martin, Miss Glitter appeared riveted. Franklin was listening with slightly drawn mouth, his long, thin hands arranging and rearranging his cloth napkin.

He pleated it, unpleated it. I returned my eyes to Mackie's neck, prepared to plunge back into my fears and my dreadful burden of love. Then my attention shot back to Franklin. He pleated, unpleated. Then he folded the napkin into neat triangles, triangles that got smaller and smaller but never less neat. His long white fingers smoothed the napkin out. Then he pleated it. Then again, the triangles. Meticulously neat triangles. Where had I—?

His eyes began to turn toward me, and I instantly looked forward, my heart thumping.

Through no great feat of ratiocination, I, Aurora Teagarden, had solved a mystery.

Franklin Farrell was the murderer.

He was folding and refolding his napkin in the same curious way Tonia Lee's clothing had been treated. It was as unmistakable as a fingerprint.

Franklin Farrell.

Chapter Fifteen

I couldn't jump up and scream and point to him. I had to force myself back down in my seat. I gripped my hands together, willing them to be still.

Charming, handsome Franklin, who'd had so many conquests they must have become boring and routine by now. Franklin, with a house we all entered only once a year for his annual party, a house that could be full of things stolen from homes he was showing.

Franklin could have had Tonia Lee just by crooking his finger, and his legendary charm could have persuaded lonely and shy Idella to do something she must have known was incredibly suspicious. How had he persuaded her to return the key to the key board, or to give him a ride from Greenhouse Realty to his house? He must have told her that he had arrived at the Anderton house to find Tonia Lee already dead – though what explanation he could have given her for going to the Anderton house at all I couldn't imagine.

Maybe he'd told Idella that putting back the key would lessen the chances of his being suspected of something he hadn't done, but Idella couldn't stand up to the heavy secret she carried, the guilt she felt. I remembered her crying in the bathroom of Beef 'N More, the day of her death. And Franklin, of course, could tell Idella was cracking. Even if she couldn't face the fact that Franklin was almost certainly the murderer, she would feel terribly conscious that she had lied to the police. And to her employer.

'Roe? Roe? Are you all right?'

'What?' I jumped.

Martin was leaning toward me, his incredible light brown eyes full of concern. His innocent light brown eyes, I thought with a swelling heart.

'Um, as a matter of fact, Martin, I don't feel too well.' People were getting up, chatting. Time to go.

'Let's get you home, then.'

Martin retrieved our coats while I sat at the table, afraid to look up for fear I'd meet Franklin's eyes. He and his date were still sitting across from me.

'Let's leave, honey,' she was saying.

'Want to stop at The Pub for a drink?' he asked, his voice warm and inviting as a crackling fire on a freezing night.

'Sure. Then we'll see after that,' she said teasingly.

There wouldn't be much to see, I thought. It was already a case of my-place-or-yours. And, my mind raced, I was willing to bet it would be hers. Franklin probably still had the vases from the Anderton place in his house. Somewhere. He'd be afraid to sell them in Atlanta, surely, with the case still so fresh. On the other hand, I argued with myself, keeping the vases in his house would be so dangerous! His car would be an even riskier place, though . . .

I slipped into my coat without even thinking about Martin, who was holding it for me.

How could I get the police to search Franklin's house?

Martin's arm was around me. 'Are you going to make it to the car?' he asked, concerned.

'Martin, I'm thinking,' I told him. He looked at me oddly.

'Honey, I'm going to get the car. I'm worried about you. I'll bring it around as quickly as I can.'

I nodded absently, and was only vaguely aware when he left.

'It was so nice to meet you,' a voice at my elbow said with routine courtesy.

I looked up at Miss Glitter. 'Enjoyed it,' I said automatically. I tried not to look at Franklin, standing at her elbow. Terry Sternholtz and Eileen came up, Terry looking very pretty in the dark blue, her curly red locks tamed into a striking hairdo. It felt strange to realize that Terry had dressed up as much for her date with Eileen as I had for my date with Martin.

'I'll be late Monday,' Terry told her boss. 'I have an early appointment with the Stanfords.'

'I'll be in Atlanta all day,' Franklin said casually. 'I'll see you Tuesday.'

But as Eileen, Franklin, and his date walked away, I gripped Terry's arm. I must not have been gentle; she looked surprised as she asked me what I wanted.

'Terry. Do you remember saying, when we were at the Greenhouses', that a self-defense course wouldn't have helped Tonia Lee? Because she had been tied up?'

Terry groped in her memory. 'Sure,' she said finally. 'I remember. So?'

'Do you by any chance remember who told you Tonia Lee had been tied?'

'Oh. Yeah, it was Franklin, next morning at the office. I get sick at grisly stuff like that, but Franklin gets into it.'

'Thanks, Terry. I was just curious.' Terry looked at me doubtfully, but then Eileen called her impatiently from the door, and she left, giving me a suspicious glance.

Donnie Greenhouse's stupidity had maybe saved his life. He'd heard Terry make the comment about Tonia Lee's being tied and realized its significance long before I did – well, maybe he wasn't so dumb after all. He'd probably been plotting some elaborate revenge against Terry, never thinking to ask her where she'd gotten that damning piece of information. All the time, it had been secondhand.

I stood lost in thought until I realized Arthur had taken my hand. His wife was across the room talking to my mother.

I was eager to tell Arthur what I'd seen; okay, napkin-folding can't be used as evidence, but at least I'd get a message to Lynn surreptitiously, an indicator that the police should look Franklin's way very quickly.

But Arthur had his own agenda, and in a particularly maddening gesture I remembered vividly from our relationship, he raised his hand when I started to talk.

'Roe, that guy is bad news,' he said, fixing me with his flat blue eyes. His voice was low and steady and absolutely sincere. 'Because of the good times we had together, I'm warning you. Get away from him, and stay away. This isn't sour grapes on my part. We've done a background check on him, and he's not—'

'Arthur,' I said with great force, to stop whatever he was going to say. I was thrown completely off-track. 'I appreciate your concern. But I am telling you that I am in love. Now, you listen to this—'

'If you won't shuck him, I can't make you.'

'You are so right—'

'But you have to know that that man is dangerous.'

'Who's dangerous?' asked Martin with a ferocious cheerfulness.

'Mr Bartell,' Arthur said, hostility in his voice. 'I'm Arthur Smith, a detective on the local force.'

Martin and Arthur shook hands, but looked as if they would just as soon have arm-wrestled.

If they'd had fur around their necks, it would have been standing on end.

'Glad I met you,' Martin said enigmatically. 'Roe, I brought the car around.'

'Thanks, honey,' I said, and Martin slid an arm around me and we turned to go to the car.

'Tell Lynn I need to speak to her,' I told Arthur over my shoulder.

'What's happening, Roe?' Martin said after we'd left the Carriage House parking lot. 'Are you really feeling sick?'

'No. But something happened tonight, and we have to talk about it.' Who else was more qualified to handle dangerous situations than Martin? He was dangerous himself. Maybe he would have an idea.

'Does it concern that policeman? Is he someone you've gone out with?'

'He's married and has a baby,' I said firmly. 'I went out with him a long time ago.'

'Was he warning you about me?'

'Yes, but that's not what I want—'

'He said I was dangerous. Do you believe that?'

'Oh, yes. But—'

And suddenly we were in the middle of our first argument, which I couldn't quite figure out. Somehow he was angry because Arthur had enough feelings for me to want to warn me off Martin, and I gathered it wasn't the warning but the feelings that upset Martin. And then also, he felt that Lizanne's engagement ring had overshadowed the beautiful earrings he'd given me, and he was mortified. And I was trying to tell Martin I loved the earrings and wouldn't have taken an engagement ring if he'd given it to me, which was completely untrue and a very stupid thing to say. If we had fallen in love like teenagers, we were quarreling like teenagers, and if we had been a little younger, I'd have given him back his letter jacket. And his class ring.

And then, just as we pulled into my parking lot, his beeper went off.

Martin said something truly terrible.

'I have to go.' He was suddenly calm.

'I have to tell you something,' I told him urgently, 'about Franklin Farrell. *Before* tomorrow!'

'I can't believe I said all those things.'

'Please come back.' I was almost crying. I'd been through too many emotions in one day, and they were seeking their natural vent.

'As soon as I handle the situation at the plant, I'll come back.'

'Wait a second,' I said as I slid out of the car. I ran to unlock my back door and ran back to the car. 'Here's my key.' I put it in his hand and closed his fingers around it. 'I have another I'll use. Come on in when you get back.'

We looked at each other searchingly. 'I've never given anyone a key to my own house before,' I said, slamming the car door and running into the town-house.

Madeleine was standing curiously in the cold draft from the door I'd left open, and she rubbed against my legs as I stood in the kitchen area wondering what on earth I was going to do.

I wandered up the stairs, pulling off my finery with little regard for my hair. I left my earrings in, and sat at my dressing table admiring them absently while I tried to figure out what to do.

What if I called the police station and said there was a kidnapped woman in Franklin's house? Wouldn't they be obliged to break in to see?

Maybe not. I could hardly call Arthur to find out.

Report a fire?

Well, the firemen wouldn't recognize the vases, as indeed most of the policemen wouldn't. Of course, we didn't have photographs of them, and my mother had only a general memory of their shape and position on the night tables.

Tomorrow Martin would be taken in for questioning if I couldn't draw attention to Franklin *now*. Day after tomorrow, Franklin would take the vases to Atlanta and sell them or drop them in the river on the way, if he hadn't done it already.

He'd be out of his house tonight, with Miss Glitter.

I stood there in the bathroom with my fists balled, trying to steel myself against the decision I was about to make.

Okay. I'd have to do it.

Thinking harsh thoughts about how incredibly stupid I was, I pulled on heavy socks and blue jeans and a T-shirt and a sweatshirt. I zipped up my black boots and found an old jacket with deep pockets. I found a knit scarf that had a hood for the head and then two long ends that tossed around the neck, which I pinned so I wouldn't have to keep fooling with them. Everything I had on was black or dark brown or navy blue. I looked like someone who'd dressed with only a tiny amount of light in the closet, just enough to pick out dark colors, but not the right dark colors. Amina would have a fit, I thought wryly.

I did keep on my beautiful earrings.

Downstairs I trudged, terrified and determined, to stuff my pockets with screwdrivers and anything that looked as if it might be helpful in breaking into Franklin Farrell's house.

I added a heavy, fist-sized rock to my collection of potential burglary tools. I'd brought it home as a souvenir of a trip to Hot Springs, and it was dark with a protrusion of clear crystal. Then I remembered a crowbar in a box of Jane Engle's tools I'd had stored in my extra bedroom.

I dumped everything into the car. It was eleven o'clock, my dashboard informed me. I am a law-abiding person, I told myself grimly. I don't litter. I don't even jaywalk. I never park in handicapped spaces. I pay my taxes on time. I only lie when it's polite. Lord have mercy on me for what I'm about to do.

That thought, from my saner self, sent me right back inside. I took a piece of paper and a pencil and wrote, 'Martin: Franklin Farrell is the man who killed Tonia Lee Greenhouse. I am going to go break into his house and get back the vases he took from the Anderton place. Eleven o'clock. Roe.' Somehow writing this note made me think I was being much more prudent, a totally unjustified feeling. But I locked the door to the townhouse before I shut it, thus burning my bridges behind me, since I'd forgotten to get my extra key and Martin now had mine.

I left my car two blocks south and one block east of Franklin Farrell's house, which was inconveniently located (for me) on a main thoroughfare, where no parking was possible. Franklin had an older home on a street that was now almost all commercial, but he had painted it an eye-catching combination of dove gray and yellow, and tricked it up with expensive antiques and gadgets until it was now one of the town's notable homes. Entrance to it was very restricted, though. Franklin entertained women there sometimes, it was generally understood, but had only one social gathering a year in his home. It was carefully planned, lavish, and invitations were much prized. Otherwise, Franklin entertained clients and other business associates at restaurants. He never asked uninvited guests in, no matter how attractive they were, a quirk of his that was much discussed and secretly envied by those who were too cowardly to do likewise.

All this I knew about Franklin. All this, and now much more.

I probably wasn't particularly silent as I stole across his backyard and up to his back door. But in that cold, who had their windows open to hear? I was shivering as I tried the back door knob, just for the hell of it. Of course, the door was locked. Franklin's car wasn't there, so I assumed he and Miss Glitter were having a good time. I hoped it was real good, and that he'd stay the night. I had no plan to conceal the break-in, because I thought I'd be damned lucky to get in at all, much less try to be clever about it. So after an attempt or two with the screwdrivers, I just smashed a pane in the kitchen door window with my souvenir rock, which I popped back into my pocket. I reached in carefully and unlocked the door. It should have opened then, but it didn't. Though my coat and sweatshirt gave my arm some protection, I became worried that the glass remaining in the frame would cut me as I prodded around inside, trying to discover what was still holding the door.

Finally I risked using my flashlight. With my face pressed against an upper pane and flashing the light up and down the inside of the door, I discovered at long last that Franklin had put a sliding bolt at the top of the door. The moment I saw it, I switched the flashlight off.

I was too short to reach the sliding bolt.

I took a few deep breaths and poked through with the longest screwdriver. I stood on tiptoes. I closed my eyes to concentrate. The tip of the screwdriver finally touched the knob of the bolt. With every bit of stretch I could summon, I pushed the bolt back.

I had to crouch down and shake for a minute when the door finally yielded. I took a deep breath, stood, and entered.

This is dumb, this is dumb, my more intelligent side was insisting as I stepped inside. Get out.

But I didn't listen. I examined the kitchen as carefully as I could by flashlight. Then, through the dining room, the hutch full of an impressive array of gleaming silver. Then into the living room, color-coordinated to a depressing degree in creamy shades, with cranberry wallpaper. The fireplace across the room was flanked on either side by windows, and matching sofas faced each other in front of them. My flashlight flicked over the furniture, the gleaming hardwood floor, and the marble fireplace. And came back to the fireplace.

The vases were on the mantle. I caught my breath at the sheer gall of it. Placed as carefully as if they were legitimate, they looked lovely on either end, with a dried-flower arrangement in between. If they'd been stashed in a closet, they'd have seemed much more suspicious. I walked up the alley formed by the two sofas to examine them more closely. These were the right ones. I remembered the pictures of rivers and valleys that had so entranced me as a child.

Hah! I could feel myself smiling in the dark, though the insistent pulse in my brain kept telling me, This is dumb, this is dumb.

And it was, too, because just then Franklin turned on the light.

'I didn't hear you pull up,' I said lamely after I swung around to face him.

'That's obvious,' he said. 'I saw a light dancing around in my living room from two blocks away, so I left my car parked on the street.' If he'd seen me through the open curtains, someone else could, too, I thought hopefully. Franklin reached out one arm casually and pressed a button. Behind me I heard the curtains electronically swish shut.

Of all the damned gadgets.

We stood looking at each other. I was wondering what happened next. Maybe he was, too.

'Why on earth did you do this?' he said almost wearily. The handsome face drooped on its elegant bones. He tossed his overcoat over the back of the sofa as though he were about to sit in his favorite chair and open the newspaper. Instead, he pulled a long, thin scarf from his overcoat pocket.

'Oh, you just carry one with you now? Just in case you run across someone who needs killing?' The words popped out before my brain could censor them.

'Tonia Lee was a piece of trash, Roe,' he said coldly. 'But she was clever enough to spot some things in my house that she shouldn't have. She was willing enough to keep quiet for some – exotic – rolls in the hay. Unusual places. Being tied up. Tonia Lee liked that kind of thing. But I got tired of obliging.' I pictured him sitting at the foot of the bed while Tonia Lee was tied to it, talking to her while methodically folding her clothes, Tonia Lee knowing all the while that she was going to die. 'A piece of trash,' he repeated.

He wasn't slotting her in a social class or giving a character assessment. He was dismissing her as nonhuman, inconsequential. On a par, perhaps, with a mole that was making ridges in his lawn. It made me sick.

'What about Idella?' I asked involuntarily.

'She was so easy to get to bed after I'd finally convinced her to just go out with me. I was glad I'd gone to the trouble of overcoming her scruples at dating a man with my reputation with women, because when I needed her to put back that key, it wasn't hard at all to persuade her. I told her it would ruin my business if I had to tell the police I'd been in the house with Tonia Lee's body. I told her I'd had an anonymous call that I should hurry over to the Anderton house, that the caller said it was Idella who was hurt there. How could Idella refuse to help me after that?' He raised his eyebrows mockingly. 'Obviously, someone wanted to frame me for Tonia Lee's death, someone who knew I'd go rushing to help Idella. It was after she had time to think that she became difficult. She sensed – some implausibility. She was scared of being single, scared of being alone; but she became even more scared of me,' said the man who was quite happy with being alone because he was so fond of himself.

'And me?'

'You're a little different,' he conceded. 'But now you know about me, and no one else does. No one else even suspects. Why did you have to do this?'

'Why'd you have to come home? I thought you were all set for the night.'

'Oh, Dorothy?' He actually thought for a moment. 'You know,' he said almost musingly, 'I just couldn't be bothered.'

He stepped toward me. I glanced at the front door, since Franklin was between me and the back door. The front door was locked and had a similar bolt at the top. I would take seconds reaching it, and more seconds stretching up to the bolt. There was no way. The doorway to my left was shut, but it might be a coat closet, for all I knew. And probably was, because right by it was an ornately carved openwork umbrella stand, appropriately holding a fancy umbrella with a long ferrule.

'I had to do this,' I began, moving slowly to my left around the end of the sofa, compelling him with all my will to watch my face and not my feet, 'because tomorrow the police were going to get Martin.'

'Martin – oh, the new boyfriend. The reason you wouldn't go out with me.' His voice held a mild interest as he came closer. 'Why are you edging left, Roe?'

I pulled the umbrella from the stand. 'Because I hope to hurt you some before you hurt me.' I gripped it determinedly with both hands, pointing the sharp ferrule in his direction.

He laughed. He really did. Wrapping the scarf around both hands in a practiced move, he held out the taut length so I could admire the shine of the blue silk. 'This is Terry's scarf. I think I'll leave it on you so maybe they'll think Terry killed you because Eileen had the hots for you. What a hoot.'

Ha ha. 'Martin will kill you for this,' I said with absolute assurance.

'Your latest honey? I think not.'

And before this could go any further, I charged at him with all my strength and yelled as loud as I could, which was pretty damn loud.

I was short and he was tall, and I was bent over in my charge.

I caught him just in the pit of his stomach. Actually, a *little* lower.

He shrieked, his arms flew up linked by the scarf, and he began to double over. I reeled back from the impact, staggered, went down on my face.

He fell right on top of me.

I fought to get him off, though the air had been mostly knocked out of me. I bucked and pushed and heaved, but he was too heavy. He was growling now, a horrible animal sound, and the glimpse I caught of his face was terrifying, if I could have been any more frightened than I was. He had apparently never been hurt before, because he went berserk with rage. He'd let go of one end of the scarf. He was tearing at any part of me he could get hold of, and I heard a rip and then some clinking, rolling sounds as one of my pockets was absolutely torn off my coat, its contents spilling out.

He grabbed my mass of braided hair and banged my face against the hardwood floor. For a moment of blinding pain my brain went dark, and I heard a cracking sound I couldn't understand. Then he lifted himself on his knees to get a good swing at my head, and I seized the second to turn over. Now I had one free arm, but he came down on the other one. When I tried to bite him, his suit coat prevented me. He grabbed my hair again and banged the back of my head against the wooden floor. I had another moment of darkness, and then with the little energy I had left I grabbed his ear with my one free hand and pulled and pulled, though he tossed and twisted to shake me off. My other arm, trapped between our bodies, hurt dreadfully, though I had no time to think about that.

I realized I was losing consciousness, the weight of him pushing the air out faster than the struggle was letting me take it in. I dug my fingernails into his ear to mark him, since I was losing, and had the satisfaction of feeling wetness under my fingers. But it almost made me lose my grip on his ear. He'd remembered the scarf now, wrapped it around his free hand, and then put it around my neck. I had the wooly scarf pinned there, though, and the collar of my coat, too. But I began to feel myself blanking in and out, like a flickering picture on a black-and-white television. My hand finally lost its grip and slipped to the floor. My fingers landed on a rough lump. My souvenir rock. I forced my fingers to curl around it, and with my last strength I swung the rock and made direct contact with the side of Franklin's head. The sound was dull and nauseating.

The weight on top of me went limp. There were some oddly peaceful moments, because of the silence, the stillness; most of all the cessation of fear. Then I became aware of hearing noise again. Was someone talking to me?

'Let go,' said a fuzzy voice, urgently.

Of what? I wondered if I was barely clinging to my life. Should I let go of it? I wanted it.

'Let go of the rock.'

It was a voice I could trust. I let go, moaning at the sudden pain in my cramped fingers.

I heard sounds, sort of – dragging sounds, and something bumped down the length of my body. Franklin Farrell's head, as someone dragged him off me. I tried to focus, but achieved only a blur.

'I can't see,' I whispered.

'It's me, it's Martin, Roe. Lie still.'

Now that I could do.

'I'm going to call the hospital.' Footsteps retreated and came back. At some point. Everything was fuzzy and blurry and vague.

'Did I hurt him bad?' I mumbled through thick lips. They also hurt. I was finding that a lot of things hurt as my adrenaline ebbed.

I heard a choked sound.

'I called the ambulance for *you*.'

'Why can't I see, Martin?'

'He broke your glasses. They cut your face. Maybe your nose is broken. Maybe your arm, too.'

'Oh. My eyes okay?'

'They may be once the swelling goes down.'

'Did – I – kill him?' I was having some difficulty enunciating.

'Don't know. Don't care.'

'Tough guy,' I mumbled.

'Tough woman,' I thought he said. I would have snorted derisively if my face hadn't hurt so badly.

'Hurts, Mar'in,' I commented, trying not to whine.

'Go to sleep,' he advised.

It was surprisingly easy to do.

Chapter Sixteen

Rubber soles against tile. Trays banging against a metal cart. A voice over a public-address system.

Hospital sounds. I turned my head.

'You're making a habit of this, Aurora,' my mother said sternly. 'I don't want to get one more call from the hospital in the middle of the night telling me my daughter's been brought in beaten up.'

'I promise I won't do it again,' I mumbled painfully.

'For a librarian, you are . . .' And her voice faded out. But when I was all there again, it was still going on. 'John and I are not as young as we were, and we need our sleep, so if you could just get beaten up in the daytime . . .' She was stomping around verbally, because ladies couldn't just stomp around.

'Mother. Am I hurt bad?'

'You're going to feel terrible for a while, but no, no permanent damage has been done. You may have some scarring around the eyes from the cuts your glasses caused, but it's probably going to fade. By the way, I called Dr Sheppard this morning to get a new pair made up. They had a record of what frames you ordered the last time, so they'll be just like your other glasses. He promised he'd have them later today. To continue – the muscles and ligaments in your left arm are strained badly, but the bones aren't broken. Your nose, however, is. Your lips are cut and swollen. Your whole face is black and blue. You look like hell on wheels. You have an engagement ring on your left hand.'

'. . . What?'

'He came in and put it on this morning – he got it right after the jeweler's opened, he said.'

I couldn't lift my arm to look. It was taped or bound somehow.

'You're not supposed to use that arm for a while,' Mother said sharply. 'Wait a minute. I'm going to push the button to raise the head of the bed.'

I opened my eyes cautiously and saw blurry pale blue walls and my mother's arm. It really was daytime. Then as the angle of the bed moved, I was able to see down without shifting my head, which felt as if it might fall off if I did so. My pale left hand was sticking out of a sling, and on it, sure enough, glittered a diamond bigger than Lizanne's.

Of course he would get one bigger than Lizanne's.

'Where is he?' I mumbled through my swollen lips.

'He had to stay at the police station this morning, to talk about the man his foreman caught stealing last night, and about – Franklin.' My mother's voice said the name reluctantly.

'There's some doubt about Franklin's bail hearing,' she went on more cheerfully, 'because you hit him hard enough to put him in this hospital – right down the hall, with a policeman in there with him and his arm handcuffed to a bedrail.'

Franklin's arm, not the policeman's, I assumed.

'You hit him with a rock, I believe,' my mother said remotely.

'Vases,' I said urgently.

'Yes, they know those are the vases from the Anderton

house. The senior Andertons had some pictures taken of their more valuable doodads and stored the pictures in their lockbox, and Mandy just now got around to opening the things she had shipped from Lawrenceton to Los Angeles. When the police here called her about the vases being missing, she mailed the pictures, and they arrived yesterday. There's proof. They'll nail that bastard.'

I'd never heard my mother say that particular word.

But I wondered if they could find proof to stick the murders to him. Besides what he'd said to me. I would have to appear in court. Again.

I heard a light knock, and my mother called, 'Come in.'

'Oh,' she said rather stiffly. 'All finished at the police station?'

Martin.

He murmured something to her.

'I'll just leave for a minute to get a cup of coffee, since you're here,' she said with assumed offhandedness.

The door swished again, and I heard him approach the bed. I wiggled the fingers of my left hand, and he laughed.

'Do you like it?' he asked quietly.

He came into my field of blurry vision then. I had a good right hand, and though any movement was not without its cost, I reached out and placed it on his chest. Then I patted my left hand with my right.

'You're cocky,' I mumbled.

This was so romantic.

'I didn't want to take any chances. For all I knew, the doctor might be a former flame who took this chance to rekindle the relationship.'

I giggled, which was quite uncomfortable.

'Roe,' he said more seriously, 'why did you do it? Why did you place yourself in danger like that?'

I was amazed he didn't know. Somehow, I'd assumed the police would tell him. Of course they wouldn't. I beckoned him to bend over with my good hand, so I wouldn't have to talk as loud.

'They were going to question you.'

'You—' He walked away from the bed, stared out the window for a minute, stalked back. 'You did that because you thought I might be arrested?'

I nodded. 'I had it from some reliable sources. I realized at the banquet that Franklin was the killer. No proof.'

'You crazy woman! He could have killed you. If I hadn't been able to settle the problem at the plant in record time, get back and read your note, find out where the hell Franklin Farrell lived . . . at least I still had the map of Lawrenceton in my glove compartment that the Chamber of Commerce gave me when I moved here. You could still be lying there with him on top of you.'

I wondered hazily what would have happened. Would he have regained consciousness before I'd managed to crawl out from under him and get to a telephone? I was glad I hadn't had to find out.

Martin was still running on. 'Did it strike you that I might be able to find the damn vases? Did you think of telling me? I would have broken into his house.'

And possibly been arrested, and lost his job . . .

'It never occurred to me,' I enunciated with some difficulty, 'to ask you.'

There was a harder, brisker knock at the door. Martin went to open it.

'It's the police,' he told me more gently. 'They need a statement about last night.'

'If you can stay,' I managed to say.

So Martin sat beside me, or stood beside me, or walked around the bed, while I mumbled my story to Lynn Liggett and Paul Allison, whom I remembered to congratulate on his marriage to Sally. He seemed a little surprised and uncomfortable. Lynn treated me like a mental case she'd given up all hope on. I edited Franklin's remarks about Terry and Eileen; no point in dragging their relationship into the limelight because of a chance whim on the part of Franklin Farrell.

Finally the two detectives seemed satisfied, if disgusted, with me, and after telling me ominously she would be talking to me again, Lynn strode out of the room. Paul Allison followed after giving me a hard look and shaking his head.

Martin did his circuit of the room again. I waited for him to calm down.

Another knock, this time perfunctory.

'Here's your pain medication. Need some?' asked a plump nurse with curly silver hair. I was delighted to see her, and the two pills I swallowed had an almost instant effect. Martin had to stomp around some more after she left, while I got drowsier and more comfortable. Everyone seemed quite angry with me today.

Finally he came to rest by the bed. My eyes met his. 'We are going to have to do a lot of talking when you can talk a little better,' he said.

We needed a change of topic.

'Talk about the wedding,' I said clearly, and coasted off to sleep.